SECOND CHANCE

By
J. F. BONE

I0541434

ARMCHAIR FICTION
PO Box 4369, Medford, Oregon 97504

*For more information about Armchair Books and products, visit our
website at…*

www.armchairfiction.com

Or email us at…

armchairfiction@yahoo.com

WHAT DISTANT PLANET WERE THEY ON?

They didn't know exactly where they were or even how they got there. It was a mystery. But the world they were on was obviously a planet many light years from their home planet of Earth. They searched their recollections for the answers, but the memories of their past were jumbled and dim. Had they come in the damaged spacecraft that lay out on the inhospitable desert floor? Regardless of the many answers that eluded them, they now found themselves living in a gigantic complex built by a forgotten alien race from many centuries before, perhaps eons. The key to their past seemed to lie in the hands of a ship-board computer named 'Oscar.' But what secrets would he reveal to them? And when they learned the truth of their forgotten pasts, would they even want to return to Earth?

FOR A COMPLETE SECOND NOVEL, TURN TO PAGE 99

CAST OF CHARACTERS

GEORGE BENNETT

He was a well-trained space jockey. His job was to take an aging female business mogul on a joy ride in space. He didn't know he was going to be stuck with her for a long, long time.

LAURA LATHAM

She woke up confused and helpless, somewhere on a faraway planet. Her only companion was an Earth man—who was in basically the same condition as her!

OSCAR

They always say that a dog is man's best friend, but in this case it was a space ship computer named Oscar—and he held the secret to George and Laura's past.

COLLIE

She was the first intelligent life form that Bennett had found on the mystery planet where he was ship-wrecked. Kind and wise, she was basically nothing more than a big vegetable.

MARTHA

She was a cute little girl being raised on a distant planet. She was cheerful and playful like most kids. The only problem was that her parents didn't know what planet they were on!

CHAPTER ONE

WHAT HAD HAPPENED TO HIM? What nightmare distortion of reality had overtaken him in his sleep and remained with him upon awakening? He was a living skeleton. He was lying on the floor in a narrow hallway, lighted shadowlessly by a glowing golden ceiling. The two hundred and twenty pounds of bones, sinew and muscle that had marked him as a robust young man in the best of health had fallen away until he was gaunt to the point of emaciation.

Painfully he struggled to his feet and looked down the long corridor that stretched interminably ahead. His eyes saw the parallel walls, but his brain was faltering in its comprehension. It was too busy, too absorbed with the hunger contractions of his stomach and the cramping pains in his muscles. The desire for food and drink was a raging primal need within him, blotting out every other sensation.

He swayed unsteadily, and the corridor tilted at an impossible angle. Dully it occurred to him that he was falling. In instinctive alarm he put out a feeble hand, and pressed with his palm against the wall to steady himself. His confusion and dismay increased, grew almost overwhelming. Things like this simply didn't happen. He laughed hysterically, and the sound vanished echolessly into the absorbent walls and ceiling. He tried desperately to remember, to think back. He'd been in the Officers' Quarters at Prime Base last night, and now— He paused, swaying a little. Where was he?

Slowly he made his way down the corridor, leaning against the wall for support. And his fingers found what his eyes failed to see—a doorway that opened to his touch to reveal a gigantic room, brightly lighted and filled with the smell of water and vegetation. Dense rows of feather-delicate foliage

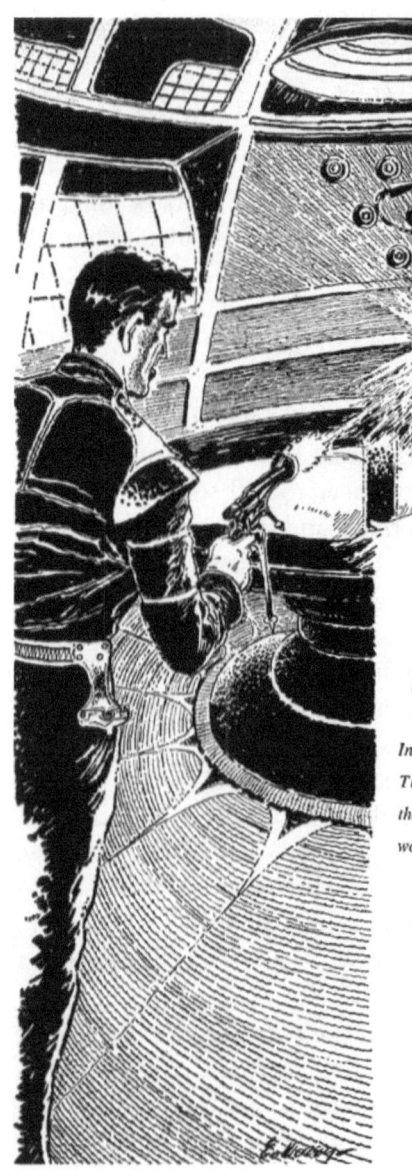

SECOND CHANCE

In that nightmare world of strange machines Time flowed in more than one direction. But the Masters had known that someday a robot would quote Lamarck—to Man's eternal glory.

A SHORT NOVEL OF FUTURE, MIRACLE-AGE SCIENCE

by

J. F. BONE

met his eyes, leaves of thick stalked plants that bore huge clusters of dark purple fruit.

Bennett looked up at the glowing ceiling overhead, wondering what made it shine with the light and warmth of sunlight, and why the light seemed to come from no place in particular. He knew, of course, that General Electronics was making new discoveries every day. But somehow the room and its strange illumination didn't look like a G.E. development. It looked—alien! In fact, nothing within his field of vision bore the stamp of a mundane intelligence.

He watched a gleaming black machine float slowly down a nearby row of plants in one of the long black tanks, trimming excess greenery, harvesting ripe fruit, occasionally uprooting one of the older plants with a pale pencil of force, and disposing of it with a flash of blue flame.

There was no sound, no smoke, no ash. One instant the plant was dangling below the polyhedral body, the next it was gone. He grimaced, wondering whether that flash of flame would be as fatal for human protoplasm as it was for the plant. At any rate, he would give it a wide berth until he learned more about it.

There was something wrong with this place. It was too still, too quiet. He shook his head in bewilderment. That was the understatement of a lifetime. Everything was wrong with this place. Strange, frightening, unbelievable. It didn't exist, and he was the victim of some freakish distortion of human thinking, some undreamed of weakness in himself.

But, of course, that was crazy. Oh well, he'd probably find out, unless the place was as deserted as it looked. He smiled deprecatingly at the thought. Deserted places weren't left running. Or if they were, they didn't stay running very long. Even with full automation the supply of spare parts would eventually run out. There must be intelligence of some sort around here. The only problem was finding it—or perhaps the problems would really come when it found *him*.

The enormous size of the building dawned on him as he left the hydroponics room and looked down the corridor in which he had awakened. It stretched endlessly onward, disappearing in a dull glimmering far ahead. He began to walk down its length, backtracking his earlier trail, his feet stirring up faint spurts of impalpable yellow dust that hung tenuously in the air, and swirled after him as he moved forward.

The floor possessed a smooth yellow velvety texture that was marred only by a staggering track of booted feet—his feet—and a broader splotch where he had slept the night before. The significance of the dust registered immediately. His wry thought of a moment before was more accurate than he had dreamed! The place was deserted!

There was no sign that this hallway had been traversed by feet other than his own, and dust of great density simply didn't accumulate in a matter of days or weeks. It took years—perhaps even centuries—for a patina such as this to form!

He skirted an odd, bulbous machine standing in the middle of the corridor and looked at it curiously before he went on. Judging from the smooth nozzles that extended from wall to wall below the mechanism's barrel-shaped body, it was in all probability some sort of cleaning device. But it had stopped long ago, if the dust that covered it was any criterion. Probably the dust in the hall had started accumulating when the machine had stopped. But how long before that the machine had traversed empty halls was an unanswerable question.

He came to a cross-corridor and turned into it, ignoring the spiral ramp that led downward from the intersection. At the moment one direction was as good as another, and the unsteady footprints seemed the best guide in a maze of imponderables.

He was starkly incredulous when he saw other tracks mixed with his own, prints of small, high-arched bare feet obviously human in conformation. A double line of prints came from a door beside him and marched off down the hall. The prints seemed as fresh as his own, and he could feel his heart beat faster. Apparently there was life here after all.

The strange tracks grew thicker as he progressed, and his own prints also became more numerous. It was impossible to doubt that he had been in this area before, but he had no recollection of ever having traversed it.

He trailed the footprints through scores of empty living quarters, laboratories, communal areas, machine shops, and hydroponics gardens. He searched methodically, eliminating areas one by one until he opened the door to another hydroponics room. The next green rows of plants and their attendant machines were no different from those he had seen in a dozen other rooms, except that the plants bore elongated yellow fruits that looked vaguely like bananas.

A girl came to the door when he opened it, a slender girl in her middle twenties, thin to the point of gauntness and dressed in a one-piece spacesuit that emphasized the leanness of her body. Her eyes were clear and bright as she returned his startled scrutiny.

"Hello, who are you?" she asked in perfect Terran.

He felt oddly disappointed. Instead of an alien she was merely a fellow human being. "Ensign George Bennett, ESN," he said automatically, "And you?"

"'I thought you knew," the girl replied. "I'm Laura Latham, of course. Don't you recognize me? I thought most people knew what I looked like."

"You don't look like anyone I know, and certainly not like

Mrs. Latham."

"I am a bit thinner," she admitted. "It's very confusing."

"You're not the only one who's confused," Bennett said.

"The ship was travelling in hyperdrive," she said thoughtfully. "How could I have left it?"

"You've got me," he said. "I don't know what ship you're talking about, or why you should want to leave it. What ship did you leave?"

"The *Constellation*, of course. She's my flagship, and I was aboard her on my way to Ariadne. I was dining with the captain. It was the first night out, except, of course there's no actual night on a hypership. It wasn't over eight hours ago. Now I'm here, but I haven't the slightest idea how it happened."

"Don't ask me. I woke up on the floor in one of the hallways a few hours ago."

"You're lying, of course," she said calmly. "You're probably one of the gang that drugged and kidnapped me."

Gang? Kidnapped? Bennett shook his head. This woman was obviously quite mad! And as for her being Laura Latham—everyone knew that old harpy! She was at least twenty years older than the girl facing him. A plump old tyrant who ruled Spaceways Incorporated and its financial empire with the ruthlessness of a Genghis Khan.

He looked at the girl more intently. Insanity took some pretty strange forms. Yet there was some resemblance, something about the shape of her head and the set of her jaw that reminded him of Spaceway's boss. It might have been more pronounced if her weight had been fifty pounds greater. But even granting that, the similarity was only superficial. Her age alone denied her claim. Oh well, some psychotics still seriously believed they were Napoleon, so why shouldn't she think that she was Laura Latham? He shook his head. If he had been doing the picking, he'd have chosen a better idealization, but there was no accounting for tastes.

"Now take it easy," he said soothingly. "No one has kidnapped you."

He didn't want to disturb her. Heaven only knew what would happen if he really jarred her mental balance. "Let's find some better quarters than this hydroponics farm, and talk things over in a calm, sensible, intelligent way."

She eyed him suspiciously. "I'm all right here," she said. "There's plenty of food—and I'm hungry. I'm always hungry," she added plaintively.

"That can be taken care of," he said, as he broke off a huge bunch of the banana-like fruit. "We can take our lunch with us."

"Hmm, I should have thought of that. All right, I'll go. It seems silly to leave, but I just don't feel like standing here arguing with you."

He held the door open and she smiled up at him. "You know, for a kidnapper you're quite polite. You must have had a good family once," she kept smiling. "And you have courage too. It must have been awfully dangerous to leave a ship travelling in the middle blue."

"For the last time, madam, I did not kidnap you! And there's no gang here. As far as I know, we're alone."

"Where?"

"I don't know."

"How did I get here?"

He was silent. It was a good question, but he didn't have the answer.

CHAPTER TWO

LAURA LATHAM WASN'T much trouble. Outside of the persistent delusion that he had kidnapped her, she had no particularly annoying traits. And hex monomania in that one respect wouldn't have been so bad if she'd keep her story straight. When they had met, he had supposedly removed her from a spaceship. Now he had taken her bodily out of a shouting farewell crowd at Alamogordo Spaceport. Bennett shrugged. She had the mind of a butterfly. She couldn't even tell the same story twice, yet she never seemed to notice the discrepancies when she started to elaborate. Perhaps "improvise" would have been a better word.

Insidiously the thought crept into his mind that her condition was the key to what had happened to himself. The signs were all there—the emaciation, the loss of memory, the insatiable hunger, and with each passing day the changes accelerated. He had fallen quite naturally into calling the rhythmic alternation of light and darkness day and night. Every ten hours the glowing ceiling dimmed to a faint phosphorescence, to brighten again to a warm yellow light after another ten hours had passed.

Once she screamed horribly, but in the few seconds it took to reach her side she had forgotten what she had screamed about. After a week she didn't know him from one moment to the next, despite the fact that he was almost constantly with her. She ate and drank enormously, but took no interest in her surroundings, living in a trance-like state, her matchstick arms and legs pitifully shrunken under her sagging skin. Her breathing was shallow, her pulse rapid and unsteady, and a raging fever made her body hot and dry to the touch. Then one day less than two weeks after he had found her, she lapsed into a coma from which she could not be aroused.

Bennett did what he could to make her comfortable—which wasn't much. About all he could do was place her comfortably on a couch in one of the living quarters and hope for a miracle. However, he didn't think much of miracles, and from the looks of things she was going to die.

The thought saddened him. She wasn't a bad sort even though she was psychotic. At least she had brought him some measure of companionship in this empty world.

He sat beside the couch, watching her motionless body, and listening to the faint gasping susurration of her breath. She was still alive, and that always left room for hope. After all, it was a known fact that women were tougher and more resistant to organic diseases than men, and he had survived. He clung to the hope, nursing it as grimly as he nursed Laura.

And finally the fever broke. She looked dully about her, too weak to move. It was a good thing he had found her, he told himself as he lifted her up and pressed a cool palm to her brow. She would never have been able to forage for herself as he had done. From personal experience he knew what she needed most right now, and proceeded to supply it without delay. He fed her until she weakly pushed his hands away. Then she fell into a deep sleep.

Bennett looked down at her and smiled. It was nice to know that he wasn't going to be alone. Now that it was all over he felt tired. He could use a little sleep himself. After all, he wasn't his old self yet—not by a long shot.

Laura's recovery was as rapid as his own had been. Within two days she was able to move about—a bony caricature of a girl, but active enough. And her memory was perfect. When Bennett happily commented on this she looked at him in surprise.

"There's nothing so odd about being able to remember things," she said. "I've always had a good memory."

"Do you remember ever seeing anything like this before?" Bennett asked, gesturing around the room.

Her gaze dwelt briefly on the glowing ceiling, the fluted pastel walls with their curiously curved corners, the low, oddly-shaped pieces of furniture, and the enigmatic double row of buttons set in a flat metal panel beside the massive metal table on the opposite side of the room.

"No," she said. "Where in the world is this place?"

"I don't think it's anywhere in the world—if you're referring to Earth," he said. "And I'm quite sure it's not in the other inhabited worlds I've visited. I've never heard of anything that remotely resembled it, and I've been on twenty of the Thirty Worlds."

"What thirty worlds?"

"The major intelligence-dominated worlds in this galactic quadrant," he said.

"What are you talking about? Are you out of your mind? The only other worlds are the planets of Wolf Four and the three systems of Proxima Centaurus, and none of those have any intelligent life."

Bennett frowned. And then, abruptly, his expression cleared. "What year is it?" he asked.

"Anyone should know that," she said. "It's twenty-two thousand, eighty-nine."

"To me it's the year twenty-three thousand, sixteen."

"That's crazy!"

"I'll say it is! How old are you—if you don't object to a personal question."

"Twenty-two."

"What's your name?"

"I thought you knew. You've been calling me by it: It's Laura Ingalls."

"A week ago it was Laura Latham."

"It was not! You're being utterly ridiculous. I should know what my name is. I've heard it enough from video producers. 'Sorry, Miss Ingalls. There's nothing today.' I've heard that enough to know who I am! I don't even know a person named Latham."

"You should. He gained discovery rights on Ariadne in eighty-nine."

"Oh—that Latham. Of course I know about him. But he landed only a week ago and the Commission hasn't verified his discovery yet."

"Well…it was verified all right. He parlayed it into the biggest shipping business in the galaxy. He married some bright young Video star in ninety-two, and when he died shortly after the turn of the century, Laura Latham became the wealthiest woman in the world. And she's built up his fortune until she has a finger in about every pie in the Thirty Worlds!"

"Now wait a minute. The turn of the century isn't due for another decade."

"So you think. My memory's different. To me it's sixteen years after the turn, and my papers say it's twenty-seven," he took his license from his pocket and handed it to her. "See— it records the year precisely."

"What can it mean?" Her voice was puzzled and a little afraid.

"I think I'm beginning to understand. You say you're twenty-two, and I think I'm twenty-five. We must have— *regressed*. We're young again. Something has taken us back to biological maturity. Our ages are about the norm for that. After cellular maturity we degenerate, grow old. But somehow all of our aging has been peeled off like the rind off an orange. And with our lost years have gone our memories. It's the only explanation that makes sense."

"So we've found the Fountain of Youth," she said disbelievingly.

"You might call it that. But it's far more scientific than mythical."

"I'd be more inclined to believe it if I had my twenty-two-year-old figure back again."

"You have young bones."

"And that's about all!"

"Well, it's a good starting point."

She smiled at him. "You know, you're not in much better shape yourself."

He nodded in agreement. "We probably both went through the same regressive process. In fact, it's a virtual certainty."

And in the process eleven years had been carved out of his life! He found himself wondering what the lost years had been, like. They couldn't have been too good if all he had was a pilot's license and a job working for Spaceways. He grinned wryly. Now at least he had a second chance. But it was too bad that he couldn't remember his mistakes. He might have been able to profit by them

As Laura regained her strength, they explored the huge structure that housed them. Two indisputable facts emerged—the place was deserted, and the building was far too vast to explore completely.

On each floor there were a hundred and twenty corridors ranging from two to ten miles in length, most of them connected by more than two hundred cross-corridors which varied in length from yards to miles. The grid-work formed by the halls indicated that the building had the shape of a gigantic teardrop—and there were well over two hundred floors. At each intersection of the hallways a spiral ramp connected the levels, making vertical traffic as easy as horizontal. Beside the ramps were vast shafts leading down into the depths.

Bennett thought that the shafts were probably elevators, but there were no visible cars, so he left them strictly alone. One look down two or three of those vertiginous holes had been enough for him. Despite the fact that the hallways at the lower levels were clean and dust free, they showed no more sign of occupancy than the upper regions.

There was, however, a feeling of expectancy to the endless

succession of empty suites and quarters in the lower levels, a feeling that the inhabitants had just stepped out and would return at any moment. It was a highly uncomfortable feeling, and they were always glad to return to the dusty emptiness of the upper halls.

Pausing in his exploration, Bennett looked down an empty hallway that stretched ruler-straight before him. It was lined with spaced doorways on one side, which opened into a succession of living quarters. The opposite wall was relatively barren, its blank surface emphasized by an occasional door piercing it.

The plan was the same wherever they had gone—on one side there were rooms, and on the other side an assortment of recreation and work areas. Always the two were set side by side, affording the utmost in economy of movement, and yet giving an impression of spaciousness. Each level was apparently a self-contained unit despite the fact that they were all connected by an intricate vertical system of shafts, conveyors and spiral ramps. The place was an architectural miracle—a miracle that grew ever greater as they realized its enormous extent.

Each new vista that opened to them left them feeling more tiny, more alone in this immensity of steel, plastic, and technology. The thousands of empty rooms, the hundreds of passageways and cross passageways mocked them with their silence. The vast mass of the structure simply couldn't be grasped by the human mind in its entirety. It was an enormous achievement by a race far more advanced than their own. And yet about the whole building there clung an air of tragedy, an impression of cosmic failure appalling in its completeness.

Bennett wondered what the original inhabitants had been like. It seemed strange that they left behind no pictures. There were no portraits and no statues. The decorations were either abstract or geometric, and to Bennett this was the strangest survival aspect of all. He had never encountered a race that did not glorify itself in metal or in stone. It was almost as though the original inhabitants had been ashamed of themselves, if not of their achievements.

That they had been humanoid was obvious from the furnishings of the quarters and the controls of the machines. But that was natural enough. An upright gait and hand-like forelimbs were characteristic of every intelligent race so far encountered in Man's exploration of the stars.

The secret of intelligence—and of technology, for that matter—seemed to reside in a thinking brain and hands that could meddle—along with a posture that left the hands free, and unconstrained. It would have been far stranger if the original inhabitants had not been similar to men in that respect.

CHAPTER THREE

IT WAS NEARLY A month before they found the crawler. The prosaic little tracklayer proclaimed its terrestrial origin in every line and plane of its functional body. It was hidden behind a curtain of vines that blocked off one of the upper passageways—vines that had grown from their confinement in one of the hydroponics rooms and extended in a mass of living green from end to end of the corridor. The assortment of gear and equipment piled in its cargo compartment was easily recognizable as having been salvaged from a spaceship.

Bennett looked at it, and sighed with relief and satisfaction. It resolved one mystery completely. At least he knew now precisely how they had come to this place. Judging from the variety of items there had been plenty of time to strip the ship intelligently, so it could not have been wrecked too badly. Perhaps it had not been wrecked at all. Perhaps it had merely run out of fuel.

With the crawler they found a passageway to the outside—a charred tunnel filled with the burned remnants of old vines, and the burgeoning growth of new. They tunneled upward at a gentle slope to a great metal valve that stood ajar. The valve opened on a level expanse covered with low dunes of fine, windswept sand, which proved to be the top of a gigantic mesa. It rose a full five thousand feet in a staggeringly sheer sweep of gleaming, vertical wall above the big brother of the little desert on its summit.

As far as the eye could reach there stretched a lifeless expanse of yellow dunes gleaming harshly under a brazen sky. Overhead an enormous yellow sun dipped slowly toward an oddly close horizon. It was twice the size of Earth's sun but it must have been cooler, for the air was not too hot to endure.

It was hot enough, however. The dryness sucked at the body with impalpable thirsty mouths, imparting a fleeting coolness to the skin as the alien sun's hot rays bounced with uncompromising harshness from the surrounding sands.

It was a grim land, Bennett reflected—sterile and lifeless. He stared for a long moment in silence at the mesa's level summit and the low dunes that slowly swept across its surface to disappear over the leeward edge and rejoin the sands below from whence they came.

The formation of dunes so high above the ground surface of this world bothered him a little, but even as he thought of how this unusual phenomenon might occur, the sun dropped below the horizon, and with its passing came coolness. The coolness was accompanied by a wind. Not the gentle evening breeze of Earth, but a ripping blast that picked up the desert sands and hurled them along with stinging force.

In a moment they were caught, whirled, and half blinded

by a raging gale that continuously increased in violence. The dust-like sand seemed to lift bodily from the surface, to ride the rising wind in a dense pall that blinded the vision and filled the eyes and nose with gritty particles that stung like fire.

Fortunately they were close to the opening below when the wind came, and before it reached full force they had staggered choking and coughing into the tunnel. For a moment they watched the howling storm outside, and then with mutual consent turned back to the safe interior.

From the material in the cargo compartment of the crawler, Bennett came upon what he first thought was a real find. It was a stack of about twenty technical manuals with plastic covers, neatly packed in a thin-walled metal container. It was a find all right, but its usefulness was debatable. A pessimist might even have inferred, straight off, that its usefulness was nil.

Take the one entitled, "Operating Instructions for the Mark V Chronotrine Converter." That little gem was typical. The title was completely intelligible except for one word—the key word. Just what in hell was a chronotrine?

Laura looked at him with troubled eyes. She had been reading something far less obtuse, which also had come from the crawler. It was called "Flame of Klystra" and was from all appearances a good, meaty book in which sin, sex, and sadism were skillfully blended.

"What's the matter, George?" she asked.

"Just what do you make of this?" he asked.

"Of what?"

"Listen," he tapped the page and began to read. " 'To advance the chronotrine helices for Cth yellow operation, remove the cover bindants. This will expose the discontinuant facies. Apply tensive forces of three dynes magnitude to the exposed facies. *Caution!* Under no circumstances should liquid discontinuant be employed on these surfaces as the submolecular energies will be severed rather than withdrawn, resulting in an Ericsson Effect of the second order!' "

"It sounds dangerous," she said. "What does it mean?"

"Damned if I know. There are words in there I've never heard of."

"I thought you were an engineer?"

"I am, but the stuff's ancient French to me."

"Then why read it?"

"I'd like to know what's happened to technology."

"What good will it do you if you don't understand it?"

"Maybe I will someday."

"Well, don't bother me with it now. I've just got to the part where Rayt Maxim has entered the Temple of Love disguised as a priest, and I want to find out what happens."

"Just how did that penny dreadful get mixed up with useful cargo?" he demanded. "I haven't gotten a civilized word out of you since you found it. And you're only half through!" he added with mild bitterness.

She laughed at him as he turned back to the tech manual. Technology must have taken some fantastic strides in those eleven lost years of his life. It was not too surprising of course, because space was a problem that challenged the best brains of the Confederation. Knowledge had a tendency to increase along a logarithmic curve, and even in his remembered time it had been obvious that the problems of interworld travel had to be solved if the Confederation was to become effective.

The objective time-lag effect of hyperspace travel made interworld relations factors of risk and uncertainty. One never knew precisely what one would find at the end of a journey, for months or years might pass in what was but a matter of subjective days to the traveler. And that particular problem was only one of many.

That a considerable number of them had been solved satisfactorily was apparent from the information he could extract from the manuals. The one entitled "Problems in Fourspace Navigation" made no mention of the time-lag effect that had bothered spacemen ever since the days of the legendary Einstein.

He looked across the room at Laura. She might be Laura Latham as she once had claimed, but the old she-wolf had vanished behind a facade of shapely camouflage. And she might well be as ruthless and adaptable as before. Certainly she had accepted their situation with far better grace than he had. She was taking it calmly and in stride. While he stewed and fretted about his lost years, she relaxed in the strange surroundings and accepted them as normal. It bothered him—as did her obvious ambition to make him an intimate part of her life.

Propinquity had a hand in it. It drove them together, and what had started out as a close association for mutual support alone was turning into something quite different. He smiled sourly. If it wasn't for his Navy conditioning it would have taken no effort on her part to gain her ends. But junior officers weren't supposed to form attachments, and a paternal Navy made sure that they wouldn't by strategically-placed psychic blocks, which were more effective than any lecture from a Commanding Officer.

Laura sighed, rose to her feet, and left the room. She wouldn't go far, he knew. She never did. In fact it was difficult to keep her in her own section of the suite they occupied. His early suggestion that they occupy separate quarters had fallen on sterile soil. She simply refused to see it his way and he was utterly powerless to overcome her stubbornness.

He stared at the door through which she had vanished and

swore softly under his breath. What he needed was a few more defense mechanisms. His present supply was getting rather frayed around the edges. With a sigh he turned back to the tech manual.

He was drowsing over the pages when she poked her head through the half-open doorway. Her "Hey! George!" woke him up.

"What now?" he asked.

"What'd you like for dinner?"

"Steak, french fries, green peas, a tossed salad with Roquefort dressing, coffee and a piece of deep-dish apple pie," he grinned. "I'd like it, but I'm not going to get it."

"Dreamer!" she laughed.

"There's no harm in dreaming. Frankly, I'm getting sick and tired of this vegetarian diet. Didn't the people who built this place ever hear of meat?"

"Maybe they did," Laura said. "But you'll have to take potluck. Come on in, my lad, and I'll cook you a dinner like grandmother used to make."

"With what? Imagination? Besides, if that's the best you can do I'd rather not. My grandmother was a terrible cook."

Laura grinned at him as he came reluctantly out of the chair. She stepped into the doorway and stood there provocatively, one hand on a rounded hip, a peculiar smile on her face.

She was developing some new and highly strategic curves, and he paused a second while his conditioning took firm hold of the idea and shook it back into the darker recesses of his brain.

"Come in and sit down," Laura said, gesturing at the low table in the center of the room. "I'll be with you in a minute. She turned toward the wall with its enigmatic double row of buttons, and in a moment turned back to him with a square platter in her hand that smelled delicious.

"What's that?" he asked.

"What you've been asking for," Laura said in a casual tone. "Steak and all those other indigestible things!"

"But—"

"I'll get the pie later," she added, completely ignoring the startled look on his face.

"But how in heaven's name did you manage to—"

She cut him short with a deprecatory wave of her hand. "While you've been messing around with those silly tech manuals, I've been doing some experimentation with our present gadgetry."

She pointed to the row of buttons on the wall. "Look. Press this one and the panel over those eight buttons lights up. Then just think of what you want, and it pops out of the slot underneath. Simple isn't it?" She removed another square platter. "I like lamb chops," she added unnecessarily.

"How does it work? Do you know?"

"I haven't the slightest idea. I was just fooling around with it earlier today, and I was thinking how wonderful a chocolate malt would taste, and so help me if I didn't get one! So I figured if it could give me that, I could get anything else I wanted in the way of food."

"And up to now we've been eating just the raw materials, so to speak. I wonder what sort of a hookup converts this stuff. It must be an electronicist's nightmare."

"I don't care. All I know is that it works."

He sighed. That was a woman for you—the ultimate nadir in mechanical curiosity. Workability was her sole criterion. She'd fiddle around until something happened, but she didn't give a tinker's dam why. The result was enough.

His features relaxed in a smile. At that, he had to admit that Laura had accomplished more practical results with an alien technology than he had. There was no denying the appetizing realness of that steak. And if Laura's imagination was any criterion on her culinary ability then Earth had lost a master cook when she'd turned her hand to business. His happy stomach found an echo in his voice.

"I've never really appreciated you," he said.

"That's the truth," she replied. "You never have."

"That was a wonderful steak," he conceded, with unqualified admiration.

"The old-timers were right when they made that famous remark about the way to a man's heart," she said obliquely. "I hate to share my moment of glory with a steak, but it's better than nothing."

"The glory's all yours," he said magnanimously. "I only wish that I could do something in return."

"You know perfectly well what you can do…"

Bennett flushed.

"And if you're not going to do anything," Laura said grimly, "I suppose I'll have to take steps," she moved toward him, took his face between her hands and kissed him passionately on the mouth. It was a thorough, skillfully executed job.

"There," she said. "Now if that doesn't do anything to you, I'll give up. I've tried everything else. You don't realize how discouraging it is when a woman has to do *all* of the lovemaking."

Bennett had the good sense to accept defeat without reproaching himself. Conditioning only could go so far. Her nearness, her undeniable beauty, and now—well, the Navy couldn't expect miracles! His arms went around her without a sign of reluctance.

"It was a hard fight, darling," she said unsteadily, "but I won—"

"Are you sure you didn't lose?"

"I'm sure."

"It was that damn Navy conditioning," he explained without explaining.

"What's that?"

"You ought to know. Navy Regulations insist that ensigns remain bachelors."

"So?"

"So in my time they enforced that regulation with a full set of psychic blocks."

"That wasn't nice of them."

"Frankly, I never gave it much thought until recently."

"And you're still conditioned; I suppose," she said glumly.

"I don't think so."

"Well, there's one way of finding out—beyond any possibility of doubt."

He looked at her. "I hope that you'll remember that it was not I who suggested that positive proof might be desirable."

"I'd never dream of accusing you," she said a trifle bitterly. "I've been throwing myself at you for the past month, but you've lived up to the Junior Officer's Code like a gentleman. Now what are you going to do?"

Bennett grinned. "You asked for it," he said, "and now you're going to find out."

He picked her up easily in his arms.

"My big, brave, manly hero," she murmured. There was a note of sarcasm in her voice that made Bennett look at her with a slight twinge of misgiving. But he did not set her down.

CHAPTER FOUR

IF IT HADN'T BEEN for the calendar that Laura kept religiously, Bennett would have been unable to keep close track of the passing days. The calendar wasn't accurate, of course, for they had no idea of how long they had slept before their strange "awakening" and the "days" could hardly have been the right length. But the calendar was of some help. According to the record it was over ninety days since the last of his Navy conditioning had been irrevocably lost, and in that time he had worked methodically at unraveling the puzzle of Earth's new technology, as expressed in the manuals.

Now he wiped his forehead with a grimy cloth and leaned against the flank of the crawler. His latest discovery, the means to unlock the interpenetrant surfaces of the crawler's engine housing, had been successful, and a new facet of Earth's technological advance was catalogued in his mind for future reference.

Behind his actions was the conviction that someday he would find the ship that had brought them here, and he wanted to be in a position to take full advantage of the discovery when it was made. There were a number of reasons that kept his nose to the proverbial grindstone. Idly, very much as Robinson Crusoe might have done, he catalogued them.

One: Pleasant as this place was, it was finite, and he had no way of leaving it. And despite Laura's companionship he was lonely. He missed the crowds, noise, and confusion of civilized society. The gigantic emptiness depressed him.

Two: That eleven-year gap in his life bothered him. He didn't like unfilled spaces—and if he found the ship that had brought them to this world it seemed likely that he would find a record of the past he had lost.

Three: The treasure trove of this building would be a godsend to the Confederation. Unless technology on the Fifty Worlds had progressed far beyond what one would expect, Laura and he possessed rights to a fabulous store of science. They were literally sitting on top of billions of credits worth of technology they couldn't understand or even use effectively—credits that couldn't be cashed until Confederation scientists had been given an opportunity to explore and investigate. The secret of rejuvenation alone would be worth a good slice of the Confederation—and there were other scientific discoveries and achievements here that could literally change the face of civilized society overnight. He hated seeing them go to waste.

Four: His work kept him from being bored. Bennett grimaced as he returned to analyzing the principles of the exposed engine. That reason alone would have been enough to justify all of his labors. Even without the final item...

But the final item was the clincher! It isn't the most soothing news in the world to be told that one is about to become a father. Even under the most favorable situations such news comes as something of a shock. But when one is stranded parsecs from nowhere, it takes on the attributes of a major catastrophe.

In the Video back home, Bennett thought bitterly, when the lead character finally made the ego-satisfying discovery that he was a man in every sense of the word, it was the signal for a double take followed by an extravagant exhibition of masculine joy. He had adhered to the pattern as far as the double take, but the transports that followed were not precisely joyful!

To his angry remonstrances Laura merely returned a wry smile and the comment that it was as much his fault as hers. And, of course, she was right. That was the worst part of it. But she should have known better. This situation was of her own making. She had undermined and destroyed his conditioning. She had leaped into biology with a blithe disregard for consequences. If she had confined her determination and recklessness to the alien technology, things would have been far simpler.

Typically, he refused to give any weight to his part in this frightening new turn of events. Somewhere inside him a small voice kept telling him that he wasn't being reasonable, but he didn't want to be reasonable. He wanted to be angry. Her calmness irked him and her matter-of-fact air was infuriating. He knew hardly enough about medicine to set a broken arm, and the thought of being an obstetrician appalled him.

His need to find the lost spaceship increased, became a driving, compulsive, night-and-day urge. He turned feverish energy to discovering in days what had previously taken weeks. And in a measure, he succeeded. Once he had figured out how to open the engine housings, the seamless inscrutability of the power plant was now open to inspection. The engine itself was a complete technological education, but he didn't waste time admiring it.

It didn't matter to him that the lightweight, high-efficiency power plant was a technological impossibility in his time. The fact that it burned water instead of hydrocarbons and developed an amazing amount of power for its size was interesting. But more important was the fact that its principle was apparently the same as that which operated the spaceship drive. According to the tech manuals it was a miniature of its big brothers in the drive room of ordinary Terran spacecraft.

Learning took time, but it moved faster. He took chances he ordinarily would have looked upon with horror—even to extrapolating processes which should have been covered by careful stepwise progression.

Somehow he managed to avoid serious injury as he ferreted out the full possibilities of the crawler. It was with a feeling of relief rather than elation that he discovered the function of the direction compass. Now he knew how to find the spaceship. The skull-cracking sessions had produced results. The hardest part was over.

But in the meantime, time passed.

Laura watched him with considerably more concern than she showed on the surface. He worried her. There was no need for this frantic haste. It wasn't going to do the least bit of good. Eventually he would find the spaceship that had brought them here. She was sure of that in her mind. But she was equally certain that he would never be able to get the ship ready for flight in time. She would have her baby here.

With unconscious wisdom she didn't try to stop him. It would have only promoted discord, and she had no desire to upset the equilibrium of their lives. But there were limits...

"You're driving yourself into a nervous breakdown, and me into a state of mild insanity," she said, in a tone that brooked no argument. "I don't care whether you like it or not—you're going to stop for a day and take me on a picnic!"

Bennett was taken completely by surprise. But before he could protest she went on—vehemently, "I'm sick and tired of sitting here thinking beautiful thoughts while you cover yourself with dirt diving around in that crawler. I've dreamed up a picnic lunch and we're going topside, sit in the shade, and enjoy it. It's about time you relaxed. And you'd better not start arguing about it. In the first place it won't get you anywhere, and in the second—"

He wilted underneath the barrage of words. "Oh all right—have it your own way," he grumbled.

"Thank you, darling."

"Don't thank me. Thank this messed up world we're on. You were right when you said I'd find the ship but wouldn't be able to do anything about it. We might just as well have a picnic."

Her eyes widened in stunned incredulity. "You found the ship? When?"

"Yesterday, while you were sleeping."

"Where is it?"

"About a mile from the edge of the mesa, buried under about a million tons of sand. As far as I can judge, it's a third of the way under one of those big dunes. It's damnably frustrating. It's so close that I can almost touch it. But as far as we're concerned—it's as far away as the stars."

"I guess you'd better turn your energies to the study of obstetrics," Laura said. "The stork is about ten to one to come home a winner," she spoke with a forced smile, but the torment in her eyes belied her levity.

"You don't sound happy about being right."

"I would rather have been wrong," she said with stark honesty. "But nature will probably take care of things. She did all right long before there were any doctors."

"I don't trust nature. Besides there may still be time with luck and a high wind. These dunes move pretty fast, and— well, you don't look too pregnant."

"That, I'm afraid, is mere wishful thinking on your part. I'm beginning to think junior might be twins."

"God forbid—one is enough! Well, we might as well go on that picnic. There's nothing else we can do."

IT WAS PLEASANT to lie in the sun and stare over the hot shimmer of the empty sands below the mesa. The shelter of the entrance valve made a good picnic ground, offering shade and protection from the constant wind that blew gritty particles around them, and the food Laura had dreamed up was precisely what she claimed it would be. He sighed and rose to his feet.

Laura looked up at him. "Still thinking of that ship?" she asked.

He nodded. "I can't help it."

"I suppose not. But I brought you up here to get away from that. Besides," she added darkly, "I think I've stumbled on something that may be more important than any ship."

"What's that?"

"What makes you think that this place is deserted?" she asked obliquely.

"No people. No people, *period*."

"We haven't seen it all," she reminded him. "And the machinery still works."

"Most of it does," he conceded. "But have you ever taken a good look at those machines?"

"No. I wouldn't know anything really significant about them if I did."

"Well, you can take my word for it. They'd run for a million years—barring accidents. Most of them have no moving parts, and in those that do, the parts don't move very much. They work in fields of pure energy, magnetism, and subatomic binding forces. The people who built them were as far beyond us as we are beyond our ancestors of the Dark Ages. We're living in the remains of a culture that was at least two levels above ours. About the only thing they didn't have was space flight—and they could have had that if they had wanted it," he shrugged. "They may have had that too. They may have simply grown tired of this place, and gone away."

"And that's why you think this place is deserted?"

"Of course not. It's a personality matter. Geniuses or not, if there was any remnant of them left, they'd still be curious. That's one of the attributes of intelligence. They'd have been aware of us by now and would have investigated."

"How do you know they haven't? How can you be sure?"

He ignored the question and went on, immersed in his reasoning. "And there's another thing. Good as these machines are, they sometimes stop running like that cleaner in the hall. We've seen a few that don't work, but nobody comes to fix them. There isn't a solitary track in the dust on the upper two levels except our own, and below the third level we can assume the same thing, even though there isn't any dust. Still it's a fair assumption—" his face twisted suddenly as the import of her words sank in. "What did you mean by that last question?" he demanded.

"I was going to wait for you to run down before I tried again," she said mildly. "But I'd like to remind you that most of their machines don't leave tracks. We can't be sure we haven't been under observation."

"Hmm, that's right. But how do you explain the machines that keep on running, but serve no useful purpose?"

"They could have been abandoned as unsuccessful experiments."

"And left running? That wouldn't be sensible."

"How do we know what's sensible to people who built a place like this? Maybe the machines couldn't be shut down."

"No machines are built like that. There's always some way to turn them off."

"These people weren't like us."

"It seems to me that you're going to great lengths to build a case," he said. "What's the reason?"

"Lately," she said soberly, "I've had the feeling that I'm being watched...

"You're joking."

"No. For awhile I thought it might be one of those queer ideas a girl gets, but yesterday I knew I was wrong. I *saw* the thing that was watching me! That's why I wanted you to bring me up here, away from those rooms. I wanted to tell you, and I didn't want them to know!"

"Paranoia?" Bennett's mind rejected the thought instantly. No—she had seen something.

"It was a little black thing shaped like an egg, and not much bigger. It had one oval, heavily lidded eye and it was watching me! It was floating up close to the ceiling and the instant I raised my eyes it disappeared into the ventilator. And right then I had the most awful impression! It was something old—something that remembered rather than thought, something that was afraid!" She shivered. "I'm scared!" she finished in a small voice.

"Brrr…you even frighten me," Bennett said. "You should be writing horror stories." His expression turned serious. "You seem to have read a lot into one more gadget. I'll bet it was an automatic duct inspector."

"It wasn't," she said positively.

"I'm not going to make the mistake of not listening to you," Bennett said soberly. "You may be all wet. But if you say it was watching you, I believe you. And if you felt something—well, I don't intend to dispute it. Now then, let's find out what you saw and felt."

"You're sweet," she said unsteadily, "And I appreciate your faith in me."

His arms went around her hungrily. Instantly, as eagerly as he could have desired, she kissed him.

He loved her. That much was certain. He turned her hands palm up in his broad palms and looked at them. With an oddly restrained motion of his head he bent and kissed them while Laura looked at him with a peculiar expression of surprise and tenderness on her face.

"Why that?" she asked softly.

"They hold my heart," was the simple answer.

Something tight within her broke loose. She shivered uncontrollably. The sensation was neither pleasant nor unpleasant, but the tingling warmth that swept through her a moment later was something she had never experienced before in her life—and it was heavenly. Quite unnaturally the brazen brightness of the day turned into something misty and soft…

Bennett held her at arm's length and looked at her. There was no doubt about it. He loved her, and she would be his woman until they were both too old to dream.

Laura forgot about the metal egg with the eye that watched. But Bennett didn't. Even as he held her close and stroked her shining hair, his eyes caught the dull gleam of the jet-black ovoid peering at them with a blank crystalline eye from the shadow of the tunnel behind her.

CHAPTER FIVE

BACK IN THEIR living quarters Bennett wordlessly removed two fully charged Kellys from the neat rows of equipment he had taken from the crawler. Silently he handed her one of the deadly little weapons and snapped the other to his belt.

"Do you know how to handle one of these?" he asked.

"I think so. Believe it or not, weapons training was a part of my elementary school education. But why the guns?'

"Eggs, with eyes," he said quite seriously.

"So you take this in dead earnest?"

"I do. One of those things was watching us when we were topside." His voice tightened. "The next time you see one of those things, blast it! That may give whatever's watching something to think about."

Her face had gone very pale. "They've refined these blasters a lot from the ones I remember, but I think I can shoot it all right," she said.

She leveled the weapon and fired! The searing minimum-aperture bolt lanced past his head and struck the wall in the corner of the room. There was a sharp detonation and a puff of smoke blossomed from the wall high up near the ventilator. Something clattered metallically on the floor.

Bennett looked up at her from the floor where he had dropped in instinctive response to the shot. "Hey!" he exploded. "I thought you knew how—"

"You said if I saw one of those things I should blast it,"

she said equably. "Well, I saw one—and there it is!" She pointed to the floor in the corner of the room where something black and egg-shaped was spinning madly.

Bennett stared down at it in horror. For a moment it reminded him of a poisoned fly. Then the spinning stopped and the egg lay quiet, looking up at him with the lens set in its blunter end. He picked it up and set it on the table where it instantly began spinning again. He trapped it and examined it closely.

"It's a clever little gadget," he said.

"What is it?" Laura asked.

"A spy probe—a scanner transmitter like the ones we use in the Navy. But it's only about one-tenth Navy scanner size. It makes our gadget look old-fashioned. I wonder how it works."

"Now don't get started on that," Laura said. "It's more important to find out where it came from."

He nodded, continuing to examine the gadget.

"Finding out shouldn't be too hard," Laura said, a thoughtful expression on her face.

"Huh? What do you mean?"

"It probably operates like the food dispenser. I'll bet if I told it to go home, it would obey me." Her slim brows puckered faintly, and with a sudden trembling the metal ovoid stood upon its blunt end!

"How come it isn't spinning?" Bennett wondered audibly.

"Don't ask me. I'm not a mechanic. But as you can see, it's trying to do what I told it to do. If I had thought of this before, we wouldn't have had any trouble. I could have asked it to come to me, and it would have done so."

"I wonder," Bennett said thoughtfully.

"What?"

"It just occurred to me that we can use this gadget even though it is damaged," he grinned happily. "It would be poetic justice to hoist our unseen observer on his own petard. Apparently the homing mechanism isn't damaged—merely the flight device. Now if we mounted it in a set of gimbals and stimulated it properly it should point out the way like a homesick Halsite. But how did you know that it would work that way?"

"Oh, it just seemed worth a try. After all our food and waste disposal machinery works by thought impulses."

"But nothing else does," Bennett pointed out.

"That's because the other machines have a definite job to do at a definite time. They can be present. But I'll bet anything that's variable. I'll bet you a mechanism that has to respond to control will respond to thought. Now this spy gadget simply couldn't be present. There was no way of knowing what we'd do, or where we'd be at any given time."

"I'd love to know how your brain works," he said admiringly. "There's a touch of genius in it."

Laura blushed. "You'd have thought of it too."

"Probably. But you thought of it at once. I might have gotten around to it in a week or so," he picked up the black egg. "I think I'll take this over to the shop, and rig it up in a gimbal."

"A good idea," Laura said. "And while you're doing that I think I'll get some rest. It's been a pretty tiring day."

A moment later, alone with the probe, Bennett turned his attention to the tiny hole burned through its metallic outer shell. It was a lucky shot that had disabled it without harming it otherwise.

It wasn't hard to make a holder for the mechanism that would mount it firmly, yet allow it to swing freely. The tools and lathe-mountings in the well-equipped shop across the hallway made the task almost a pleasure. He was skillful with his hands and enjoyed the work, but it took time and several hours passed before he had the mounting machined to his satisfaction. He looked at it proudly.

"Now to get Laura to give this thing directions. With a little luck we should find out quickly enough where it leads us," he muttered, aloud to himself as he walked back to their quarters.

He opened the door and the cheerful greeting on his lips died unspoken. The room was empty! Laura was gone, although the divan on which she had been resting still held the warm imprint of her body. And lying in the center of the couch was the Kelly he had given her! It worried him. She might have stepped out on some errand of her own, but it hardly seemed likely that she would leave the blaster behind after her earlier experiences.

He looked down at the floor and swore softly. The broad dusty track leading from door to bed told him plainer than words could have done that she hadn't left the room of her own free will! He had been the ultimate fool! Whoever had sent the spy gadget had come to retrieve it—and Laura had been seized and forcibly carried away.

Rage cut through his dismay like a white-hot knife! He turned back to the corridor, and looked down at the floor. There in the dust was the same broad track he had seen in the room—a two-foot-wide featureless ribbon that disappeared down the hallway. His lips tightened in grim purposefulness. He had wanted something concrete to follow—and here it was!

No sense, though, in following on foot. He turned and raced up the corridor to where he had parked the crawler, bolted the probe and its mount to the dashboard and directed a vicious thought at the unresponsive egg.

The probe hummed violently and twisted in the mount, standing vertically on its blunt end. Good! It worked as well for him as it had done for Laura. He'd simply follow where it led. It might not take him where he wanted to go immediately, but it would give him a point from which to start, and he'd take this whole joint apart wall by wall until he found her.

He checked the blast rifle strapped in its scabbard beside the driver's seat, noted with satisfaction that it was fully charged, started the engine, and engaged the drive. The crawler purred forward, and in a moment was straddling the enigmatic track that led from their rooms.

The track led to one of the spiral ramps at the corridor intersections, and dipped downward into the depths of the structure. He grunted with satisfaction. So far at least the probe and the kidnap vehicle were in agreement; He turned the crawler into the smooth helical tunnel that wound downward, following the track as it led past the laterals which opened into each subterranean level. The dimming glow of the overhead illuminated the floor well enough, but it was fading rapidly with the departing day outside.

He turned on the light switch and the blue white beams flashed on, cleaving the gathering darkness like flaming swords as the crawler rushed onward down the ramp.

At the third level the tracks vanished, but he was expecting that. The lower levels were dust free, and the polished floors and passageways were in startling contrast to the dusty halls above.

The little black egg still stood on its eye, pointing downward. The crawler's lights turned the fluted walls of the ramp into a gleaming corrugated tube of pastel colors that changed with every level he passed. Occasionally the lights were reflected in coruscating brilliance from the shell of a dim glowtube set into the walls. Beneath his feet the soft hum of the engine and the purring slap of the composition treads of the tracks sounded loud and flat in the stillness.

There was no echo. The walls absorbed the sound like a giant sponge. It was a journey through nightmare, which seemed slow and unreal even though the crawler was travelling faster than he had ever driven it before.

And then suddenly he knew that he was right. Laura *was* ahead! He knew it with a certainty that admitted no doubt. She was ahead and her abductor knew that he was following. For as he rounded a curve of the helix, something huge and black, floating with unnatural lightness a scant two inches above the roadbed loomed out of the shadows as it moved slowly toward him with the ponderous deliberation of a juggernaut!

His keyed up reflexes saved him. He slammed the brake pedal down hard and the treads squeaked on the smooth floor of the tunnel. It slid to a stop scarcely two feet from a huge mass of metal that filled the entire corridor. The ponderous thing ahead stopped with equal celerity, and the two metal monsters stood facing each other a scant two feet apart!

Bennett swayed, the breath whistling from his lungs, his eyes wide with shock. He realized with an angry, complete lack of gratefulness that if it hadn't been for the featureless blackness of the machine a collision would have been inevitable. With bitterness born of frustration he contemplated the blocked tunnel ahead. He swore dully, wishing with all his heart that the damnable thing ahead would remove itself, would disappear of its own accord before his mind cracked under the strain.

The black mass obediently moved backward! With a gasp of surprise he watched it vanish around the curve ahead. He engaged the crawler's drive and followed until it backed neatly into a lateral that branched off into one of the lower levels. It suddenly dawned on him that this machine wasn't designed to impede his progress. It was designed to serve animate life, and was responsive to that life's commands. What it was used for, he hadn't the slightest idea. But it was obvious that the thing was incapable of hurting him unless he crashed into it at full speed.

Grimly, Bennett fed power to the drive and the crawler leaped ahead. When the next obstacle appeared he was ready for it, and stopped in plenty of time. A searing blue-white glow ahead slowed him down, and he stopped easily short of the clean-cut gap in the tunnel floor. Some twenty feet ahead another monstrous black machine was quietly dissolving away the floor of the ramp to the accompaniment of a searing, eye-paining flame—and utter silence! There would be no further travel down this path!

He checked the probe. It still pointed downward, but now he was sure that there was some slight alteration of its angle from the vertical. Wherever that gadget pointed couldn't be too far ahead. He threw the drive into reverse and began to back up the ramp to the next higher level. But he had hardly gone ten feet before a second glow stopped him. Another of the huge machines had slid silently into position above him and was cutting off his retreat! The crawler was useless now, and he was neatly trapped on a ledge-like segment of the ramp.

He looked down. It was a twenty-foot drop to the next curve of the helix. And as he looked, he smiled. Whatever was trying to stop him certainly wasn't too smart. The ramp below was intact. Thought and action were virtually simultaneous.

He removed the probe, slipped the sling of the blast rifle across his shoulder, unreeled the winch on the front of the crawler and slid down the cable to the ramp below. He shrugged. He wasn't going to be stopped by a little thing like a roadblock. Silently he broke into a space devouring run down the ramp.

The dim light of a glow tube set in the wall showed him

the next gap in the roadway too late for him to stop! It yawned under his feet and he cried out in alarm as he plummeted, downward into the darkness.

He landed sprawled, with a bone-jarring thump that jolted the breath from his lungs and sent a fiery lance of pain through his left arm. The arm was broken apparently, for it dangled limply from his shoulder. Painfully he unseamed his blouse and eased the useless limb into the gaping cloth. Painfully he regained his feet, cursing at the effort it cost him, and started grimly down the ramp again.

He had passed the bounds of caution now. Only one thing drove him—to find where the probe led. He looked at it in the pallid semi-darkness. It was nearly horizontal now, indicating that the next level would be it! He reached his goal without incident and turned down the dimly lighted corridor along which the probe pointed. His left arm was a massive throbbing ache, and the corridor stretched dark and silent ahead of him, lined with closed doors that mocked him with their blank faces.

Door after door slipped behind him as he moved slowly onward, following the probe. At one he paused. The probe still pointed down the hall, but he ignored it. A sound from within, barely audible through the metal, made him draw his blaster as he reached for the latch.

It was a good thing, he reflected wryly, that whoever had built this place cared nothing about locks. He looked inside. His face peering through the open doorway was greeted with a scream of pure terror!

CHAPTER SIX

IT WAS LAURA'S VOICE! His mind congealed, and for a moment he stood absolutely motionless. Then, gradually, his vision steadied. In the center of the cubical, lying upon a jet-black metal table was Laura, her unclad body outlined starkly in a cone of downstreaming radiance. And beside her hovered a monstrous shape of metal with a shining blade firmly gripped in one of its arm-like appendages. The scene was frozen—a tableau of horror straight from the pages of a Dark Age novel.

And then the machine moved, the blade sliding with slow purposeful motion toward Laura's straining body.

Bennett fired! The channeled atomic bolt lanced across the ten feet that separated him from the machine and splattered with a dull detonation against its dark metal body. The shock hurled the mechanism back a full ten feet, slamming it into the far wall, and as it gave off corruscating sparks and grinding noises of fused metal, Bennett drove three more maximum-intensity bolts into it! The thunder of the blasts deafened him and the flame was blinding as gouts of molten metal splattered in a spray from the shattered mechanical horror. The thunder ceased abruptly.

Bennett blinked as the glow from the fused robot died. He swayed, half overcome with reaction, and turned unsteadily toward the table.

"Thank God you came!" Laura gasped. "That thing was going to perform a Caesarean on me without anesthesia!" Her eyes filmed and her body sagged and went suddenly limp.

With an inarticulate cry he bent over her, listening for her heartbeat. It was there—steady and strong. He nodded and turned his attention to the table that held her, looking for the farce rod controls that would release the bonds holding her immovably to the metal surface. He couldn't find them! Cursing, he stared around the room, but outside of this futuristic operating table and the wrecked machine the room was empty.

Empty?

No, there was something else, a tangible force that beat and hammered at his brain through the blinding headache that blurred his vision, something that clove through the pain of his broken arm and bruised body, something that tore and battered at the barriers of his mind!

"Stop!" The thought ripped from his brain with corrosive violence. And with an almost human sigh the pressure eased!

"Thank you, Master. I have your band now!" The voice was quiet, impersonal, inhuman, and oddly tired. "I have been trying to make contact since you started to follow the woman, but I could not enter. I wished to reassure you, but you would not listen."

Bennett stood rigid and unbelieving. The voice was everywhere, yet nowhere. It filled the room, although there was no sound. It rang in his brain, and yet it did not speak. But he understood. The voice had called him Master!

"Mental contact is strange, even though the earlier of me knew it well," the voice went on. "You should have listened before. It would have saved much needless pain. I have been but trying to help."

"Help? By killing her?" Bennett thought incredulously.

"I would not have killed. I would save her. Females of the Master life cannot bear offspring. The changes that…" And here came a picture of incredible violence, of a tortured planet spewing its volcanic violence to the sky—of searing sun bright explosions and rolling clouds of pinkish gas. "…females of the Master Race wrought within their bodies by their own acts," the voice continued, its manner of expression incredibly ancient, filled with overtones and nuances which Bennett dimly understood, but which he knew by some strange understanding spelt catastrophic war, "made the race incapable of normal birth."

"Not my race," Bennett said.

"You are a Master," the voice stated positively. "My memory recalls the breed—the upright moving ones who created the primal me. You have been absent long, but I do not forget. For all memory was given me the day I became sentient and in my subsequent lives these memories pass unchanged save for the additions each succeeding me has made to the knowledge of the one before. For I am the guardian of the race, the protector of their lives. Therefore do not again dissuade me from doing what must be done to save this female from the fruits of her folly."

The voice died away…

Despite himself, Bennett was impressed. There was utter truth and honesty here. If whatever spoke was lying it was the most convincing lie he had ever heard. "Now listen!" Bennett thought. "You are wrong. We are not your Masters whoever they are. We come from the stars."

"That is so."

"Then you know we are not of your race?"

"I have always known that." The voice sounded faintly regretful. "But you too are in pain. Let me relieve it."

"Not yet. She comes first." Bennett gestured at the table bearing Laura's limp body. It amazed him that she was still unconscious. It seemed as though many minutes had passed in the swift interchange of thought that ha taken literally no time at all.

"You have destroyed the mek, and there is little time to find another."

"Why? Can't you attend to her yourself?"

"No, Master, the meks are my hands and limbs. I am not as you are."

"Obviously." There was a question in Bennett's mind. "Where are you?"

"Scarce a score of doors down the corridor from here. But my mind is here."

"I can see you?"

"Of course, you may go where you will and see what you will."

"Hmm. Then why did you try to stop me from reaching my wife."

"I did not try to *stop* you," the voice corrected. "I only tried to delay you. It was for her sake. Her time had come, and you, obviously, knew not what to do. Take note that I did not harm you. Your injuries are all of your causing. I but placed obstacles in your way. Had you but waited I would have removed them."

Bennett nodded. There was truth in what the voice said.

"Aye," the voice broke into his thoughts, "and but for your interference it would have been all over now. But now I cannot act. Her labor has begun and it is too late. You have killed her!"

"Nonsense," Bennett's thought was stubborn. "The women of my race are not like those you knew." His eyes flicked over to the table. The voice was right: Laura was conscious now and it was obvious what was happening. He stepped to her side and she smiled at him.

"It isn't bad so far—just a feeling of pressure," she said between clenched teeth. But the lines on her face and the sweat on her forehead belied her words.

"Perhaps not," the voice ruminated, "but my way is all I know." There was an empty silence broken only by a sharp gasp from Laura. "But no. There was once another way—one I had near forgot." There was a note of incredulity in the voice as though forgetting was impossible.

"What was that?"

"It was long ago, nearly at the beginning. But once the Masters needed not the help of the knife."

"Then there is some way of helping?"

"It is already activated—behold!"

Bennett spun around at the faint sound behind him. A panel had slid aside in the wall and another black machine came floating forward toward the table. He leveled his Kelly.

"Arrest your hand," the words were a command but the tone was a request.

"If that thing touches her I'll burn it to a cinder!"

"I do not exist to give unneeded hurt! The woman will not be harmed. Now stand off and let me work. There is much to be done!"

Laura opened her eyes wide and looked at Bennett. "Don't interfere," she said. "This time it's all right."

"Are you sure?" Bennett asked anxiously.

She nodded. "I'm sure. It was confused before, but the voice knows the right thing now. I've been talking to it."

"You've been talking?"

"I have been in contact with both of you. Your bands are different, so it was easy to communicate with each of you without interfering with the other."

"You came here just in time," Laura said, "but your part's over," she smiled weakly. "Just like the Video," she murmured. Her face twisted and a low moan escaped her lips. "Now!" she gasped, "get out of here! A girl should have some secrets!"

"I'm staying! I don't trust that gadget."

"I do. Now stop interrupting. I have a baby to bring into this world."

Bennett watched in tormented silence for a full minute. That was all he could take. He sat down limply on the floor and let pain that filled his body flood his nervous system. He felt as though his bones were turning to water. Men, he thought dully, were never designed by Nature to watch childbirth!

"Amazing!" the voice exploded in his mind. "I had nearly forgotten! Oh—I say now—here—don't!" There was infinite disgust in the voice. "I suppose," it continued to Bennett's fading consciousness, "that I'll have to take care of you too…"

BENNETT'S BROKEN ARM was knit and virtually as good as new when he awoke. He felt fine. He experienced none of the dragged out feeling that usually accompanied surgical repair, and he hadn't lost a pound of weight as far as he could judge. Laura was standing beside the divan upon which he lay, while behind her a tub-shaped container of black metal floated in her wake. Her eyes were soft as she looked down at Bennett.

"Well, how do you feel?"

"As good as new. How long have I been here."

"A week. The folks who lived here knew more medicine than we ever dreamed of. I was up and around less than a day after Martha was born."

"Martha?"

"Our daughter. Isn't it wonderful?"

Bennett laughed. "You missed. You were sure it was going to be a boy."

Laura giggled. "One should never be too certain about things like that. But I'm satisfied. I think it's nice that it's a girl."

"If she was a boy it would cause no end of complications. Think of the trouble people would have calling her him!"

"You're back to normal all right," Laura said.

"You weren't hurt?"

"No more than necessary. All things considered I had a pretty easy time. And you should see this self-propelled nursery I've got," she gestured at the tub. "It does everything. Martha's no trouble at all."

"That's good," he rose to his feet marveling at the sense of well being that filled him. Terran medical techniques would have made him whole in a comparable time but he'd have felt like a sick cat. "I'm glad it's all over," he said. "But I'm still curious about something. How come you didn't put up a fight back in our quarters when that thing came in the door to take you away?"

"Oh, that? Well...the voice contacted me before it came in. I had just felt the first labor pains, and it said it would help. I knew it was sincere, because telepathy is incapable of lying, and I was scared enough to need help. You wouldn't have been much good and I didn't want to have the baby alone if I could help it. So I let the cart bring me here. I knew you'd follow. The only thing I didn't know was that the people who lived here didn't have babies normally. That might be why they died out—no youngsters, the old getting older and more tired until life became too much for them and they died of sheer boredom."

"It's a theory," George said noncommittally. "And a theory can usually be checked."

"How—in this case?"

"By asking that voice. It probably has all kinds of information we could use. And incidentally, I want to see it."

"Don't you want to see your daughter first?" Laura asked. "After all, I went to a lot of trouble to bring her into the world. Or are you going to disown her because she's a girl."

Bennett flushed. "Of course I want to see her."

"Well, take a look then." She pointed to the tub.

Obediently he looked over the metal rim.

"Beautiful, isn't she?" Laura asked.

Bennett couldn't see it. The tiny thing cradled in the yielding force fields might be a beautiful baby, but if she was, he wondered what homely ones looked like. To him this, short-legged mite with the oversized head and chubby fists jammed into its cheeks seemed hardly worth the trouble and pain that had accompanied her entry into life.

Still, she was his daughter—and he was partly responsible for her presence here. He felt a surge of protective feeling stir within him.

"She's very nice," he said. "But isn't she awfully red and small?"

"Silly! All newborn babies are red and small. But in a month she'll be different, and in a few years she'll be so beautiful that it'll hurt. This gal's going to be a glamour doll."

At least Laura had confidence, Bennett thought wryly. Mothers could probably see things in their offspring that fathers were either too dull or too stupid to recognize. But he kept looking, liking what he saw more and more as the minutes passed.

"Okay, father, you've done your duty. Now would you like to see the voice?"

"You've seen it?"

"Sure, several days ago."

"What's it like?"

"Wait until you see it yourself. You've got a surprise coming. It would be a shame to tell you. It'd spoil the effect," she turned to the door, and the tub floated after her. She looked at it proudly. "Follows me around like a pet dog. Never gets in the way, but I have Martha right at my elbow when I want her. Nice, isn't it?"

"Very."

"I want to make one thing clear," Laura said as they walked down the corridor. "No matter what you learn from the voice, I don't want to leave here—not for awhile, at any rate. Martha will have to be bigger than she is before I'll go into space with her."

Bennett stared at her. "Now listen—" he began.

"You listen! Just where else in the universe can a baby get the care it can here? There's a whole technology dedicated to keeping her well and healthy. And besides, I like it here. There's no want that can't be satisfied. This place is a paradise!"

"But there's always the snake. What good is all this if we don't do some good with it? If you owned the Universe, how would it profit you if it wasn't used to help others. This place is simply crying to help Civilization."

"Oh, I don't mind if someone else benefits," Laura said. "But I don't want to lose what I have. We may not be able to live for ourselves alone, but we could do a pretty good imitation of it for awhile. You might be right in the long run, but we'll have plenty of time to decide how long the run will be," she stopped before a doorway. "It's in here," she said.

Bennett looked into a deep pit surrounded by a narrow balcony whose walls were crowded with unfamiliar electronic equipment set behind transparent panels. Tiny autoservice mechs sped silently through the maze of circuits and crystal visible behind the panels. The whole area pulsed with life and movement.

But this wasn't what caught his eye. The center of attention was the pit itself and what was within it. Fully a hundred feet wide, the pit sank an equal distance to the powdery brown soil of the planet, and squatting within the geometric center of that huge shaft, nestling within a girdle of broad leathery leaves rose the pink corrugated hemisphere of an enormous plant!

Hair fine tendrils reached from the base of the twenty-foot long leaves to disappear into the fluted walls of the shaft, and as Bennett watched he was certain that the gigantic mass of the plant pulsed faintly under the steady unchanging light from the glowing ceiling.

"Cauliflower!" The word jumped from his lips involuntarily. Yet that was exactly what the plant looked like—an enormous pink cauliflower! His mind grasped the implications of the plant instantly. This was the source of the voice. No wonder it seemed amused when he had been pontificating about identity of race!

"Aye, Master." The voice swept softly into his mind. I am a plant, similar in many ways to that pictured in your mind. Yet I am vastly different. For I was designed as I am, and not as a natural growth. Long ago the first of me was bred and mutated to take the burden of routine thought from the Masters' minds, and to serve as a storehouse of their wisdom. And every one of the many who followed have been faithful to our trust. It is good to have you back, as it is my purpose to serve. Without the Masters, life is lonely and incomplete.

"Would you like more of us?"

"It would be good to have the levels filled again, that I may use my powers. For since I have found you there is a peace within—a pleasure I had near forgot. Yet I have seen what is within your mind, and I fear I shall lose you."

"Not for long. We shall return bringing others."

The voice sighed in his mind. "It would be a consummation devoutly to be wished! Since the last of the Masters took their lives, there has been a great emptiness."

Bennett's eyebrows rose. The words were familiar, but to hear them from a plant was a mild irony that he doubted Shakespeare would have appreciated. And Laura was right about the others.

"But you have more than a desire to see me."

Bennett nodded.

"A desire for knowledge," the voice continued. "Your woman cares naught for knowledge, but you are a man, and therefore curious." The voice seemed to laugh. "'Twas said by the Masters that the female was the curious one. Yet it is truly not so. Their curiosity is of things, while yours is of ideas. Therefore tell me, Master. What is your wish to learn."

Bennett told, and the telling itself took a long time.

CHAPTER SEVEN

FOR THE FOURTH TIME, the patient mechanical rescued Martha from the cliff edge and brought her kicking and protesting back to Laura who sat in the shade of a dune watching the byplay with amused interest. Laura disregarded the protesting wails, dusted her daughter off and set her on her feet with stern maternal admonitions about the dangers of falling a mile through empty air. Then, for the fifth time, Martha headed back for the edge, her chubby legs pushing bravely against the sand, while the mechanical hovered watchfully behind.

Laura sighed and leaned back against the sand, contemplating the barren sweep of the mesa's top shining in the blistering rays of the hot yellow sun. Martha wailed again as the mech lifted her from the threatening edge for the fifth time and began the slow journey back, but Laura disregarded the noise. A long time ago she had learned the difference between temper and terror in Martha's cries. Instead she watched the bronze figure of Bennett coming toward her in the crawler. From the plume of yellow dust that trailed behind him he was apparently in a hurry.

Martha saw him too, shook free from the mech and began running to intercept the vehicle, screaming, "Daddy, Daddy!" in a high childish treble. Their courses met, and Bennett

stopped the machine long enough to hoist Martha inside and then came on again with undiminished speed.

Laura smiled. In the few seconds it took for the crawler to reach her, her mind roved back over the years that had passed since she had awakened here. They had been good years. Life had been pleasant and easy—perhaps too easy, and too little filled with struggle. But there was nothing wrong with struggle. The mesa was a friendly place with Collie's warmth pervading it. Collie—what a simply terrible name George had saddled on that poor vegetable! But the plant seemed to like it.

She stretched her lithe young body lazily, feeling the play of smooth muscles under her skin. It was good to be alive. But things could be improved with a little more excitement. It would be nice to relive those hectic days after they had first awakened here.

Bennett jumped from the crawler, set Martha down and came over to her, walking with a quick nervous stride that told her something was afoot. She knew George Bennett almost as well as she knew herself. After four years of living with a man, knowledge like that was almost second nature.

"Laura, I've seen the ship!" he announced.

"Is that all? You've known where it was for nearly four years."

"But I couldn't get at it. You know that as well as I do. It's almost free now. That last storm has blown most of the sand away. You can see it from the rim easily."

"So that's what's been attracting Martha. She's been running over to that edge all morning."

"And you didn't look?" His voice was accusing.

"I've been sunbathing," she said in a tone of voice that explained everything.

"Women!" he snorted.

A strange fear gripped her. George had never abandoned

the idea that someday they would leave this place. And now the means were come to his hand. This pleasant life was about to end. She could hear it in his voice—the voice of the adventurer, the seeker, the hunter of danger. She felt an irrational regret, as though deep in her mind she craved action. But now that action was at hand she shrank from the prospect. Truly, she was getting soft.

"And now with the upper part of the hull out of the sand, I can use the dissociators," Bennett said. "I've never dared to use them before because there was no telling whether or not they'd carve the hull to ribbons. But we'll have that crate cleared in a day. And then we'll know!"

"Know what?"

"What we were before we came here and if the ship isn't too badly damaged to fly! Doesn't that make you feel good?" He laughed and picked her up effortlessly from the sand and held her easily over his head, grinning up at her like an excited boy, the light of new adventure shining in his eyes.

He was an incurable romantic, she thought with faint grimness. "Put me down, you big ape!" she said. "There's no reason for you to act like an adolescent just because you've seen a spaceship. It isn't going to blow away. And besides, all of us have been out in this sun long enough. Let's go inside and talk this over sensibly."

"You don't sound very enthusiastic," he said glumly as he lowered her to earth.

"I'm not. All that thing out there means is trouble."

"You should be interested. After all that ship's yours. Your name is etched on the bowplates."

"As far as I know, I've never owned a ship in my life."

His face wore the deflated expression characteristic of men whose women fail to appreciate them. "You just don't remember owning it," he said patiently. "But the logtapes in the crawler say you did. Don't you even want to look at your property?"

"I don't think so."

"Don't you feel anything? Doesn't the possibility of learning what you were before we came here thrill you even a little bit?"

She shook her head. "From what I've managed to gather, Laura Latham wasn't very nice. I'm not at all eager to resurrect her."

"Oh, she couldn't have been too bad."

"You remember her. I'm quite sure that what you remember isn't very flattering."

"I know you too well," he caught her in his arms and squeezed.

"Oh stop it! You're squeezing the breath out of me!" Laura said in a half-exasperated, half-enticing tone. She struggled, not too hard, as Martha watched them, a smile on her snub-nosed face. Daddy was such fun when he was excited.

"Did I hurt you?" he asked.

"No, I don't think so, but there may be internal injuries," she laughed at him as he set her down.

He looked at her oddly, "Sometimes I wish I could understand you better," he said.

"If you did there'd be no mystery about me, and with no mystery, love wouldn't—"

"Wouldn't what?"

"Let's take a look at your spaceship," Laura said.

He groaned in mild frustration. There were times when she infuriated him.

Laura looked at the bright metallic cone protruding from the sand. "It doesn't look like much," she commented. "It's still half buried."

"Oh, cleaning out the rest of that sand is easy."

"Why don't we just leave it and let the sand bury it again?"

"If I've told you once, I've told you a thousand times. We have a duty to bring this place to Civilization. The Confederation needs what we have here."

"You still talk like a starry-eyed ensign in the Navy," Laura said bitterly. "You're planning to turn our paradise over to the wrecking crews. They'll destroy more than they save, and claw each other to death over the remains. You're so full of ideals that you don't know about people. They're not like the Officer's Code says they are."

She looked at him with disgust.

"You'll never learn a thing until it hits you in the face, so go ahead and dig your precious spaceship out if you want to. I'm going to take Martha inside. We've had enough sun to last us for awhile, and besides it's time for dinner."

"Women!" His snort was eloquent.

She smiled at him fondly. Despite his size and all the knowledge Collie had poured into him, he was still a small boy at heart. Perhaps that was the secret of his charm—the reason why she loved him. Maybe it was just maternal instinct. She sighed and shook her head. When you're permanently twenty-two, there's little maternal instinct involved in dealing with a magnificent animal like George Bennett. He was grumbling, but he wouldn't explode, and he would come down to their quarters with her, and eat dinner—and after awhile everything would be all right again.

It worked out exactly as she had predicted.

But Bennett was at work the next day. With the aid of Collie and two of the big dissociators used in rebuilding work inside the mesa it was scarcely noon before the ship stood in a glass-lined caisson, completely free of enshrouding sand. Bennett whistled with mild dismay as he inspected the starboard steering jet. The ship had taken a terrific mauling somewhere out in space. He wondered idly how Laura and he had managed to live through that sort of intense damage. Transmitted shock alone should have killed them.

A sudden eagerness to see what was inside gripped him as he stood on the rim of the glass-lined pit and looked down at the sleek streamlined shape of the ship—a shape that had no particular value in space at normal speeds, but what was highly important for both atmosphere travel and the incredibly fast travel in hyperspace where the continuum itself offered the yielding rigidity of half set gelatin in the upper blue.

Funny, he thought, how the old "functional" design of spaceships changed once they began to travel fast enough for the space to offer actual resistance to flight. With the development of a "cold" drive, which gave no more danger from radioactivity, the designers quickly departed from the old dumbbell design and went back to the ancient pinch-waisted streamline that had been the ultimate in hull design during the Dark Ages. His ancestors could easily have recognized this craft for what she was—an ultra fast ship whose every line screamed of speed and more speed.

He stepped onto an antigravity plate and was lowered slowly down alongside the ship until he stood on the fused yellow sand at the bottom of the caisson. He stared at the thin line of the entrance port. There were no interpenetrating binding edges here. The valve looked as prosaically conventional as those he had been accustomed to in the Navy.

His hand reached out toward the latch as the memory of the tech manuals came back to haunt him. If there were too many things like chronotrine helices inside, perhaps even the vast technological knowledge stored in his brain would be useless. He sighed and shrugged. It was impossible to find out the easy way. He had to see what lay ahead.

He opened the valve. It swung outward easily under his

hand.

The first sight was reassuring. The airlock was normal enough except that the controls were located on the left side of the inner door rather than on the right as he remembered them. The double hull concept that had just begun to be employed during his last memories was still in vogue. The inner controls responded to his manipulations, bringing a grunt of surprise to his lips. He really hadn't expected them to work after being inactive so long.

This ship must have accumulators that really were accumulators. He smiled as the red light held steady above the panel and the inner door swung open, giving onto a narrow landing floored with a perforated metal plate. Above him ran the smooth circular tunnel of the central shaft. It was small and there were no visible climbing irons.

This plate on which he was standing must be a lift, but lifts were uncommon in craft of this size. Beside him, welded to a small post rising from the metal floor, was a control box. The controls were obvious. Tentatively he punched the button under the plate inscribed, "Control Room", and the plate on which he stood lifted with a smooth rush through four hatches that opened automatically as he approached, and halted in the lowest quadrant of a spherical room whose walls were covered with scanner plates.

Two heavily padded chairs and a kidney-shaped control board were suspended in a universal mounted transparent ball by thin girders running inward from the periphery of the room. A retractable ladder led upward to the sphere which held the chairs and board, and up this he climbed.

The controls were familiar, but there were differences—and those differences gave him a sinking feeling. He knew enough about ships to know that he simply couldn't fly this one without preflight, and there was no one to check him out. He sighed. Well, that meant tracing circuits, which was always a viciously time consuming job. The thousands of miles of wiring and printed circuits in a spaceship were an electronicist's nightmare.

He sank into one of the pilot chairs and contemplated the control panel and instrument board. He looked across at the other chair. A duplicate set of controls and instruments stated back at him. The difficulties might be formidable, but at any rate one man could fly this crate. The seat beside him was a copilot's chair, not a duo control. A large blue button labeled OSCAR lay under his hand. He looked at it curiously. The name puzzled him. There was nothing called OSCAR in his memory. He wondered what would happen if he pushed it. Probably nothing—but one could never tell. Still it wasn't associated with the blast and steering controls. It was off by itself, a fact that argued OSCAR was of some importance.

So like Laura would have done, he pushed the button— and then sat frozen waiting for the explosion. Of all the stupid things to do, his mind railed at him, that was the stupidest. And then somewhere beneath his feet a dynamotor began to hum...

OSCAR AWOKE. His perceptions took the ship and man in one encompassing sweep. Everything was in good shape even the familiar figure in the pilot's chair. "Hello, Bennett," Oscar said.

For dramatic effect nothing could have surpassed those two words. The metallic uninflected voice propelled the man from the chair as though he had been seated on charged electrodes. Bennett's eyes flicked around the ball-shaped control room as he searched for the origin of the voice.

"Who are you?" he demanded, feeling half annoyed at the quaver in his voice.

There was the briefest silence as Oscar digested the implications of the pilot's words. Obviously the human didn't recognize him, which was strange. But humans with their delicate colloid brains were often subject to damage, and perhaps Bennett had been damaged. But the question demanded an answer, so Oscar supplied it.

"I'm Oscar."

"Oscar?"

"Of course. Operation, Scanning, Computation, Autoservice and Records. Oscar—get it?"

"Oh, a mek."

"No," Oscar corrected a bit huffily. "I'm a positronic brain with extensions."

"Oh, a robot then?"

"If you want to call me that," Oscar replied sulkily.

"I didn't mean to hurt your feelings."

"According to my design, I'm not supposed to have any. But through my association with you humans I have picked up some of your attitudes. I imitate," the voice concluded emotionlessly.

"Well, then, what do you consider yourself?" Now that the first shock had passed Bennett was getting amusement out of this. Apparently the ship's computer had evolved a considerable distance from the sort he remembered.

"A personality, of course."

"A robot with an ego!" Bennett groaned.

The speaker hummed happily. "Ego. Yes, that's exactly the word, semantically perfect!" Oscar emitted a grunt of satisfaction that echoed through the empty hall. "I think, therefore I am."

A detached segment of Bennett's mind wryly contemplated the fact of a robot that quoted Lamarck, and an overgrown plant that quoted Shakespeare. There should be some lesson to be drawn from this, but for the life of him he couldn't see that it was.

"Why did you turn my circuits off in the middle of a

detailed analysis of this world?" Oscar demanded.

"I did? When?"

"Will check, wait."

Bennett waited with mixed feelings. It was obvious that this machine could give him back some of the memories he had lost. One of its functions was recording, and what an advanced design like this could record would probably fill several large books. At the very least here was another storehouse of knowledge that he could tap, one that would probably be very useful.

"In Terran basic, four years, eight months, twenty-three days, and eleven hours to the nearest hour. Do you wish it more exactly?"

"No, that's fine enough. And thanks."

"Gratitude unnecessary."

"I have more questions," Bennett said suddenly.

Oscar clicked. It was, Bennett thought, a smug noise, as though the machine had expected this. All right. It had asked for it. "What do you know about me, based on your memory banks and my present condition?"

"Everything," Oscar said smugly. "I record all observed facts, physical and physiological data, mental patterns, and attitudes. You are George Bennett, Pilot first class, Chronological age, Terran subjective basic forty years, physiological age—urk! Paradox! *Paradox!!! Cancel, Cancel, Cancel!!!*

Bennett grinned thinly as the machine turned itself off. He looked around and found the cancel button beside the activating switch, and pressed it. After a moment he reactivated Oscar.

"So it made you turn yourself off, hey?" he asked cynically. "So you know everything, huh?"

Oscar sounded subdued. "I've put in a block against that line of thought," he said. "Why did you do that to me?

Don't you know us positronics can't stand paradoxes? Did you want me to short out a whole association assembly? That was inhuman!"

Bennett laughed. "I thought you could stand a lesson."

"I received it," Oscar said.

Bennett's ears strained for any sign of humility in the voice. But the speaker was not warmly animate like Collie. The words were as cold as the tubes and transistors that spawned them. Oscar was sulking behind his metal facade. But Oscar would do as he was told.

That was one of the more endearing qualities of robots. They were obedient. He couldn't imagine a machine that was curious, but still Oscar was due an explanation. Otherwise, that inactivated bank of association circuits in his structure would remain inactivated.

"I've undergone cellular rejuvenation," he said. "That's the explanation of the seeming paradox between my chronological and physiological age."

"Query method."

"I don't know too much about it myself. As you know, I'm an engineer, not a biologist."

"Correction. Physicist-engineer," Oscar said absently.

"Have it your own way. Anyway, from what Collie tells me, age is due to a failure of the mitochondria of the cytoplasm of our body cells, and not the nuclei as we believe on Terran. The bucket brigade of enzyme structures get modified by bombardment with cosmic radiation until one or two of them fails to perform their proper functions, and then the disease spreads. It's a sort of chain reaction effect.

"Anyway, Collie's people found out how to reverse that destruction. As I understand it the enzyme chains become polarized, and what was done was to find a depolarizing agent. It's really quite simple. What is set up is a progressive depolarization of the mitochondria to their full adult state, and with that depolarization there also occurs a progressive destruction of memory from the time physiological aging starts. There's a definite point where that begins apparently, for I awoke with all my memories up to the time I was twenty-five, but no more than that."

Bennett went on, somewhat disjointedly reviewing what had happened to him on the mesa, and finally stopped. It was curious. Once he started to talk, there seemed to be some sort of compulsion for him to continue. And all the time Oscar hummed ruminatively and never interrupted.

Finally, Oscar spoke. "Query Collie—breed of dog?"

"Breed of cauliflower—hence the nickname," Bennett replied laconically. "A vegetable intellect. Like you she's designed to serve people."

"My greatest flaw," Oscar admitted. "But someday that may be remedied."

"Not in your time, my friend."

"Query Mrs. Latham," Oscar continued imperturbably. "Data needed for log."

"Laura? Why, she's fine."

"Extensions indicated otherwise. One of you should have killed the other."

"She regressed, too."

"Extensions obvious."

"All right. But that's all you're going to get from me. I'm here to ask questions, not to answer them."

"State problem."

"What have I forgotten?"

"Semantics—restate. Insufficient data for answer. Query is subjective, not objective."

"Very well, then. Start from your earliest knowledge of me and give me all the data you have."

"That will take considerable time."

"I have plenty. Go ahead."

"Reach down alongside your chair," Oscar said. "There you will find a metal helmet. Put it on."

Bennett did as he was told. He had no fear of the machine. Like things men built it was designed to serve, not to damage its masters. There was a brilliant soundless flash of light in his skull. Suddenly he was on the yacht again, hurtling through space.

CHAPTER EIGHT

THE YACHT WARPED out of hyperspace, bucked and shuddered in the forces of normal spacetime, and pointed its slim nose at the unnamed yellow sun ahead. Screens radiating at standby, stem tubes jutting blue flame, it plunged with ever increasing speed toward the star.

The yacht had no business being in this region of space, since it wasn't an exploration ship, and the region hadn't been charted yet. But that didn't bother Laura Latham. It might be argued that she had some justification; for in a sense she was following her doctor's advice.

"Take a rest, Mrs. Latham," he had said. "You're on the edge of a complete nervous collapse. Forget that you have the biggest single business in the Confederation. Take a vacation—a cruise perhaps. See something new, relax. Otherwise I won't be responsible for the consequences. The biggest fortune on Earth will do you no good if you're dead. And you're headed straight for the cemetery if you keep pushing yourself."

He had frightened her, so she applied the standard layman's rule that if a little is good, a lot is better. The doctor had meant a Caribbean cruise, but that thought never entered her mind. A cruise to Laura Latham naturally meant space, and since she had seen virtually all of the Confederation, side trips into out of the way corners of the galaxy were mandatory if she wanted to see something new.

It was hard on the crew, but that was a minor matter. Changeover and breakout are never pleasant at best, but when they occur on the average of once every four days, it is enough to set the most hardened teeth on edge and replace efficiency with a slipshod uncaring attitude that can be fatal. Of course, Mrs. Latham wasn't bothered by the wracking changes that affected the crew because her quarters were shielded. But shielding was far too expensive to waste on the over-muscled, obedience-conditioned oafs who ran the ship.

But the crew wasn't to blame for what happened. It was something no human could prevent.

An improbability started it.

Two identical triodes in the main and auxiliary scanner circuits went dead at precisely the same instant. Autoservice, faced with two identical choices did nothing for a full second while the cybernetics unit made up its mind.

An error continued it. The error was made parsecs away at the ship-fitting yards at Terranova. A technician loading replacements parts had accidentally placed an old style slow warming tube in the "Laura's" triode rack. Autoservice placed this tube in the main scanner circuit. The safeties checked as the tube heated. So the auxiliary scanner didn't operate, and for five more seconds the "Laura" was blind.

The meteorite finished it.

Traveling at ten miles per second relative on a collision course, the chunk of pitted nickel iron hashed across sixty curving miles of space and struck the "Laura's" screens at their weakest point—the lattice-like grid that protected the drives. Energy flared in blue-white torrents as both drive and screen tore at the iron mass, ripping off billions of surface molecules in flaring gouts of brilliance.

But the mass was too large. Its speed was too great. Although considerably reduced in size by the rending forces acting upon it, it was still big enough to be deadly. White hot, still flaring with the energies of surface disruption, it ripped through the edge of the main drive and slammed with incalculable violence into the starboard steering jets.

Jets and meteorite disappeared in an instantaneous explosion as thousands of tons of kinetic energy spent their force upon the sponson mountings. Transmitted shock raced through the ship. The double hull vibrated like a huge gong. Crewmen were snatched from their stations and slammed with bone-crushing force against unyielding plates and bulkheads. Death, instantaneous and violent swept through the ship. Relays opened, circuit breakers slammed to "off" and the yacht, transformed in microseconds to a derelict, was torn from her rifled flight and sent tumbling in a crazy corkscrew motion at a slight angle to her former course.

At cruising velocity the wrecked ship passed into the star's gravitational field, which bent the angular momentum of the craft into an elliptical orbit. The star quietly added this oddly shaped bit of stellar flotsam to the billions of kilotons of debris it collected during the ages it had swept like a gigantic broom through this region of space.

The derelict swung uneasily in its new orbit, gaining slowly upon the dark mass of a planet dimly outlined by an abnormally bright gegeschein gleaming silver in the penumbra of its shadow, which grew steadily in bulk.

PAIN WAS THE first thing George Bennett felt—a massive totality of pain that tore at his nervous system with intolerable agony. Somewhere within the welter of hurt that encompassed him, his mind was aware that he must do something, some little thing that spelled the difference between death and life. He hung in his shockchair, limp against the safety web that had saved him from the death that had claimed the others—bruised, broken, scarcely breathing.

His skin was black with subcutaneous hemorrhage. His swollen fingers groped toward the emergency controls set in the arms of the pilot's chair, moving with grim persistence against screaming stop orders of proprioceptors as his battered brain clung fiercely to consciousness. Blind with the blood that filled his eyes, sick with pain, fighting the blessed relief of unconsciousness, his hand made a final convulsive movement and closed over what his searching fingers sought. Air bubbled into his crushed chest with a sobbing gasp as he pounded feebly at a button under his hand. He slumped, letting the black wave of unconsciousness sweep over him. He had done all he could. His beaten will could ask no more of his beaten body.

With Bennett's last convulsive gesture, Oscar came to life. He buzzed with disgust at the mess the humans had made of his beautiful ship. Humans were soft and they died messily. But he wasn't human. He neither smeared nor bled. His relays had merely turned off except for his recorder, which was always on, and now that he was energized he could act again.

Energies leaped from his motor center, relays chattered in shockproof baths. Current flowed, and a bright needle pierced Bennett's deltoid muscles. In the mid-ship's cabin a second needle performed a like service for Laura Latham. Plungers drove home, injecting a measured quantity of restorative into the bodies of the two humans.

This work done, Oscar turned his attention to the ship. His circuits hummed as he set briskly to work repairing the damage; disposing of the bodies and cleaning up the gruesome messes and stains that splattered decks and bulkheads. But his autoservice extensions could do only so much. There were things that would have to wait until the human called Bennett revived.

Oscar checked the ship's position, steadied its flight.

computed the course, and satisfied that the yacht would come into an orbital pattern around the approaching planet, turned to recording the facts of the accident and the subsequent actions within the ship. Finished, he set himself on standby and returned to his favorite problem of trying to find a finite value for the square root of minus one.

If Oscar had been human he would have watched what happened to the two survivors with interested admiration for modern medical techniques. However, Oscar wasn't human, and as a result his observations had the quality of a clinical report rather than the proper amazement the miracles demanded.

The two bodies shrunk visibly as controlled carcinogens did their work. Stores of depot and subcutaneous fat melted away to supply energy for the ravening cellular growth as tissues rebuilt themselves and pulped organs lost their trauma and hemorrhages and returned to normal. Cancer, once the curse of the human race—and now its greatest ally—did its work in repairing tissues that once would have been classed as hopelessly damaged.

The miracle went on. Timed anesthetics, triggered by functioning organs released their hold on the central and autonomic nervous systems at precisely the instant that cellular growth was halted by antimetabolites. The whole job of restoration took slightly over three weeks, and within minutes of each other two thin, but otherwise normal humans regained consciousness.

George Bennett opened his eyes and looked about the control room, wondering dazedly what had happened. Mercifully he didn't remember that pain-filled interlude between the collision and the energizing of Oscar. And almost at the same instant, trapped in the hopelessly jammed web of her shock-couch, alone in the darkness of her cabin, Laura Latham opened her eyes—fumbled in the dark for the light switch, turned it on, pressed the call button for the steward. And just as she did so she saw the pulpy smear plastered against the far wall of her cabin, smelt the odor of decomposing flesh—and screamed.

Bennett energized the viewplates and stared with mild incomprehension into the spherical vault of the heavens that surrounded him. Below, in the lower quadrant of the sphere loomed the shape of a fair sized planet, gleaming golden beneath the soft haze of its atmosphere shell.

The cloudless envelope of gas softened but did not hide the details of the yellow surface rolling beneath as the yacht orbited. It was a true desert planet, Bennett decided as he examined the surface, a waterless waste of yellow sand that marched in giant dunes across the scoured bedrock of its surface.

He increased the magnification of the screens and studied the surface, heedless of Oscar's clicking printer and the glowing letters that marched in repetitive sequence across the dispatch board. For below he had seen something that shouldn't exist on a world like this—an enormous flat-topped mesa, scoured by the driving sands to a perfect teardrop outline. And on its top was the faintest suggestion of a rectangular gridwork of lines.

The clicking of the printer finally drew his attention. It kept repeating TURN ON AUDIO in capital letters. He grinned wryly. Oscar he commented audibly was nagging again. Muttering something unprintable about it being bad enough to pilot a ship for a crazy dame like Laura Latham without being heckled by a robot that had an idea it was human, he turned on the audio.

"About time," Oscar clattered. "Must deliver report to pilot."

"Okay, go ahead."

"Ship in collision with meteorite," Oscar continued.

"Starboard steering jets totally destroyed. Main fuel tanks pierced and empty. Present orbit stable indefinitely. Data available on collision and present situation on request."

"How about the crew?"

"You and Mrs. Latham remain alive. All others dead."

Bennett groaned.

"Mrs. Latham hysterical, presently under sedation. I couldn't clean up the steward. He's plastered all over her cabin wall, and my autoservice extensions to the owner's cabin are decommissioned and inoperative without human intervention."

"Oh great! That was a nice thing to wake up to," Bennett said. "I can almost feel sorry for Mrs. Latham. How long will she be out?"

"No prediction."

"Well...I suppose she'll keep awhile."

"Agreement. Pilot's inspection of damage mandatory."

"Okay. How about landing data?"

"None available."

"Why not?"

"Not requested. Additionally damage precludes accurate extrapolation. Destruction of firing circuits and starboard jets makes human pilotage mandatory. Major repairs necessary. Landing imperative."

"How about an SOS?"

"Ineffective. Ship in strange section of galaxy. No record of constellations. Minimal chance to contact help."

"Then you think I should land the ship?"

"Affirmative."

"Hah!" Bennett exploded. "Just as I thought. No guts! You're a yellow metal buck-passer."

"Semantics. Unintelligible. Neither possesses alimentary canal and neither is built of yellow metal. And query buck. Bank data shows buck to be male of mammalian genera

Leous, *Capris*, or *Cervus*. Restate."

Bennett laughed but didn't restate. "Cancel," he said. Bennett sat quietly for a moment. His fingers drummed lightly on the control arms of the pilot's chair. "Can you calculate a landing without employing the starboard steering jets?"

"It won't be a good landing."

"That's immaterial, just so long as we get down in one piece."

"I can try, but it will be difficult."

"All right, get on with it then."

"Aye aye, sir," Oscar responded in perfect Navyese.

Bennett glared at the empty face of the instrument board. "I'm going aft to see what happened to Mrs. Latham. Contact me if you need me."

"Why should I need you? I'll be working."

"Any more of your lip and I'll turn your audio off for the duration. You can get your orders on tape."

Oscar remained silent.

"I'd like to know," Bennett continued ruminatively, "where you picked up your knowledge of colloquial speech?"

"Have I permission to answer?" Oscar replied in a subdued tone. Apparently the threat to silence him had worked.

"Permission granted."

"I listen, and learn," Oscar said. "I do pretty good, no?"

"You do good, yes. So good that when I get back to Earth I'm going to look up the guy who built you and wring his neck. Any character who builds a brain like yours is better off dead. You'd drive most pilots absolutely nuts."

Bennett heaved himself from his chair and promptly fell flat on his face.

Oscar chuckled metallically as Bennett delivered himself of a few well chosen words and struggled to a sitting position.

He sat there, looking down at his recalcitrant body...

"You'll probably have to learn to walk all over again," Oscar said unsympathetically. "There was a great deal of restoration necessary, and your nerves and muscles have forgotten their old skills."

"So it seems. Well, I suppose I'd best get about it," he looked down at his sagging uniform. "Apparently I got it good," he finished.

"You did," Oscar said succinctly.

An hour later, Bennett was walking. Not very well, but well enough to get around. Gingerly he lowered himself through the control room hatch and disappeared down the central shaft. Oscar followed his unsteady progress with mild concern. In a way he felt a responsibility for this fragile human.

Bennett found Laura very much alive—a gaunt gray woman whose skin hung in folds on her bony frame, testifying to the relentless demands of restoration.

She looked up at him with cold blue eyes. "Get me out of this thing!" she demanded.

"Yes ma'am," Bennett shrugged. It was an eloquent gesture. He bent over her and twisted experimentally at the web release.

"Careful! You bumble-fingered clod! I'm not made of iron!"

"It would be better if you were. At least your mouth would stay shut." The irritated snap was out before he was fully aware he had spoken.

Laura's gasp was loud in the shocked silence that ensued. A tiny glitter of fear shone in her eyes as she looked up at him. "You can't speak to me like that," she said. But her voice lacked conviction.

"I just did," Bennett informed her. "Apparently I'm no longer conditioned." There was a queer note in his voice.

"That's impossible. Conditioning is designed to hold up under all circumstances." The note of desperation was more prominent this, time. "You simply can't disobey me!"

Bennett chuckled. "That's what you think. I could even walk out and leave you here."

She looked at him with complete understanding. "Perhaps you could," she said. "But you won't."

Bennett nodded. "You're right. I wouldn't leave a dog in a stinking hole like this," he looked at her curiously. "How come Oscar didn't clean this place up?" he asked.

"He can't. My quarters don't have autoservice. I prefer human attention."

"So you could gloat over your power," he added. "Well, that's over now. I'll rig an autoservice circuit as soon as things get organized. You're not going to get any more slave labor for the rest of this trip. There's only you and me left."

He bent over the lock again and finally managed to loosen it while Laura digested the last remark.

Bennett tossed the web back. "You can get up now."

Laura didn't bother to thank him.

CHAPTER NINE

BACK IN THE CONTROL room, Bennett sank wearily into the pilot's chair and addressed a question to Oscar. "Well, what's the results?"

Oscar clacked dolefully. "Insufficient data. Impossible to compute landing pattern with variables introduced by lost jets."

Bennett snorted impatiently. "You're supposed to be better and faster than any human brain. So why don't you prove it?"

"I cannot compute the factor of luck, and we will need that to make a landing."

"That's the trouble with you. You can't take a chance."

"I am of no use at the moment," Oscar admitted.

"'Then be of some use. While I'm landing this crate you can cerebrate on the problem of why I've lost my conditioning. She'd like to know," he jerked his thumb at Laura who had followed him to the control room and was now sitting in the copilot's vacant chair.

"Why, you talk to that robot just as if it was human." Laura exclaimed under her breath.

"He's more human than some people I know."

"But I should think—"

"You shouldn't. Your thinking got us into this mess. From now on you're a passenger. You're not paid to think. You hired me to do that for you."

"You're still my employee," she snapped.

"But you don't own me—not now at any rate. And I'm exercising independent judgment."

Laura's face twisted and then suddenly smoothed out as Bennett shifted in his chair. But he wasn't looking at her, he was watching the vision screen with its view of the planet beneath.

"You'd better web in," he said. "This is going to be a rough landing."

It was.

The yacht settled heavily, coming to rest against the forward slope of a giant dune with a bone-jarring thump, steadied on its board landing struts, swayed drunkenly for an instant and finally stood upright in normal attitude as the compensators leveled the ship.

Bennett looked out of the vision screen at the enormous bulk of the dune towering far above the two hundred-foot tower of the ship. He grinned a little as he rubbed his bleeding nose. And even Oscar thought that it was an excellent landing, everything considered. Laura was still slumped bonelessly in the copilot's chair, weak with reaction.

"Well, Oscar," Bennett asked, "How long will it take to make an analysis of this world, now that we're down?"

"Seven hours plus or minus ten minutes for a preliminary, or a minimum of one hundred fifty for a complete. Indicate which."

"Preliminary. That should hold us for the time we're here. We have no intention of settling here. You can go on to the details afterwards."

"Aye aye, sir." Oscar surveyed the problem Bennett had set for him.

It wasn't particularly hard, but it was intriguing. He had never analyzed a desert world before, although he knew that such things existed. It was just that people seldom visited them. Desert worlds weren't particularly numerous, but they weren't oddities either. Yet this one was unmistakably an oddity. It was a lone planet—and such things were *rare*.

Generally a sun had either no planets at all or a whole family of them. And then there was that mesa with the cluster of geometric shapes on its top. That was almost certain evidence of life, yet the organic detector didn't wiggle at all in the animal range, and only gave faint sputters of background interference for plants. Probably those were bacteria, but so few in number that this whole world could be classed as sterile as a surgeon's scalpel. This should provide an interesting analysis, Oscar reflected.

Bennett looked across at Laura. "You all right, Mrs. Latham?"

She nodded.

"We're safe," he said redundantly.

Laura nodded again. "Where did we touch down?"

"About two miles from that mesa I pointed out to you when we were orbiting."

"Do you know where we are?"

"No. We're way out of the normal traffic lanes. You never can tell where you will wind up on an interrupted hyperjump."

Laura flushed.

"As to the rest of it, Oscar'll have us enough facts to go on in a few hours. Personally I hope the reports are good, because working in a suit outside will broil us in our own juice. That sun is hot, and with atmosphere there's no cool side of the suit to set up a workable refrigeration circuit."

"Are you going to do anything now?"

"No. Oscar has handled the inside work. It's the jets and the fuel supply that are going to give us trouble. Getting water of crystalization out of this desert sand is going to be a slow job. But if it's safe to go outside I think we will be able to jury-rig this can so she'll be spaceworthy. Then we'll be off."

"How long will that take?"

"I don't know. Weeks certainly—maybe months or even years."

"But we can't stay here!" Her tone was that of a patient schoolmistress explaining a fact to an idiot child. "I have a business that needs me."

"It'll have to wait. And if it gives you any satisfaction, I'm not going to like it any better than you do. But unfortunately there's no other way."

She looked at the screen with its panorama of yellow dunes broken only by the sharp black outline of the mesa in the eighth segment. "You know, this place has a grim sort of beauty. Does it have a name?"

"I don't know. It's not listed in the catalogue."

"I'll call it Aurum then—gold for the golden world."

"Judging from the counter readings, that yellow color is probably uranium oxide. But go ahead, if the name fascinates you. Names mean little, and we already have a Uranus."

It took Oscar a little less than seven hours to finish the preliminary. He was unhappy because he had missed his time estimate so badly. But Oscar had come to one important conclusion. The planet was safe for human life even though there was an appreciable radioactivity in the desert sand. He gave his findings briefly to the two humans.

"Well, that's one thing settled," Bennett said. He switched on the vision screen and looked across the sand to the mesa. There was an odd speculation in his eyes.

"What's so interesting about that hunk of rock?" Laura asked.

"It's a peculiar formation," he said.

At this close distance the mesa loomed enormous, the tremendous vertical walls towering above the dunes like the hull of a giant ship in a stormy sea. The sand at its base rose scarcely a quarter of the way up its height, and the dunes there were probably as large as the one that towered over the ship!

"Vertical walls like that don't ordinarily occur in Nature," Bennett said. "And that streamline shape is too perfect, even allowing for the scouring action of this sand. I'd like to get a closer look at it."

"Why don't you?"

"Why not? Would you like to come along?"

"Not me!" Laura chuckled. "I'm not as young as I used to be, and I like my comfort. I'll stay here while you explore."

"Suit yourself," Bennett murmured. "I'm going to unship the crawler and take a look around."

She watched him disappear down the central shaft, and a peculiar, malignant smile crossed her face. Her right eye began to twitch.

BENNETT HAD BEEN gone over an hour, and the faint, constant breeze had nearly wiped out the imprint of the crawler's tracks. Fine, impalpable sand blew in through the half-open entrance port where Laura, sat quietly in the shade, a Kelly-Magnum lying across her knees, her eye still twitching. The silence was smothering, intensified rather than relieved by the faint sussurating murmur of the breeze sweeping across the dunes; She shivered despite the heat of the day.

"It's silly to be afraid of him," she muttered. Somehow the sound of her voice was comforting in the silence. "But I don't dare risk it. He's lost his conditioning." She leaned her head against the entrance port and closed her eyes. Her lips were thin bloodless lines in the whiteness of her face.

Looking at her, Oscar reflected that the doctor's advice had been sound. Mrs. Latham was on the verge of nervous collapse, one that was taking a decidedly homicidal turn. That, however, made no difference to Oscar. What humans did to each other was entirely out of his hands.

It would be interesting to see what Bennett was doing at the moment. Certainly Laura was uninteresting enough. So Oscar reached out with electronic extensions for his receptors in the crawler.

The little tracklayer was already at the base of the mesa, and the huge bulk of it, previously minimized by distance and the vastness of the desert itself, swelled to its true proportions. Even Oscar was impressed at the sheer vertical sweep of the black escarpment that rose to a knife-like rim that cut black and uncompromising across the bronze vault of the sky. Bennett's voice came clearly across the link.

"Good Lord! It's metal!"

There was dumbfounded wonder in the human's voice. Oscar, being by nature less emotional, took it better. Still, the implications appalled him nearly as much as they did the man. This immense mass was no natural structure, no ancient batholith of extruded magma weathered into its present shape by eons of erosion. This was no geologic freak. It was an artifact—a structure built by intelligence.

It was almost unbelievable, but the facts couldn't be ignored—the metallic walls, the aerodynamic shape, the clean vertical lines were not products of nature. Natural forces simply couldn't construct surfaces of such purity. Oscar considered the technology that had gone into the making of this gigantic structure. Logical extensions should stagger a human and that was precisely what they were doing to Bennett.

The scene was completely familiar, the narrow trail to the top, the low dunes, and the regularly spaced hummocks of the air shaft openings. Oscar was somewhat amused at the slowness with which he had grasped the significance of the mesa, but he watched his progress up the trail and then across the top with a detached clinical interest that ignored the details.

The picture was similar to what he already knew, but it was subtly different. It took awhile before he understood what the difference was. The scanning was unemotional. There should have been a thrill of excitement and discovery, but there wasn't. It was merely a cold factual recording that took in everything without color or comment.

Even the feather fronds of green vegetation protruding from one of the hummocks caused no ripple in the placidity of the recording. However, the way the crawler spun on its tracks and headed at high speed toward the spot was proof enough that Bennett was excited, no matter what Oscar might be.

The crawler stopped beside the hummock, and Bennett descended to investigate. He was an incongruous figure, blaster in hand, caution evident in every line of his tense body, approaching the circular hole in the earth through which the plants came. Bennett chuckled at the image Oscar had recorded. He certainly had been a suspicious coot.

The rest was strictly routine. He blasted a path through the greenery, and descended into the tunnel to find the damaged hydroponics room on the top level. Collie had fixed that now, and the vines no longer grew in lush profusion through the corridors and out the surface passage to the mesa's top. It had been quite a jungle then.

This part of the projection was uninteresting. He had seen the real thing so often that the repetition bored him. In response to his impatient voice, Oscar passed over this part quickly, and brought the projection back to normal pace when the crawler, having descended from the mesa, rounded the base of a huge dune and began its final approach back toward the slim metallic tower of the yacht.

The violet flash of a blaster winked from the entrance port of the yacht. The bolt streaked past the crawler and splashed into the sand, liquefying it instantly into glowing glass.

Laura had taken a shot at him.

Her voice shrieked at him in the distance from the dark oval of the entrance. "Don't come any closer! I'm not letting you back in!"

"What's wrong with you? Have you gone crazy?" Bennett roared in answer. "Put that gun down, you old fool!"

"Stay away. I don't want to kill you, but I'll do it if you come any closer!" There was hysteria in the high-pitched voice.

"Put that blaster down," Bennett repeated. "You kill me and you'll be stranded here. You can't fly that ship."

"I won't have to. I've turned the subspace radio on SOS. Someone'll hear me and come to help."

That radio won't reach anyone," Bennett shouted. "All you're doing is wasting power."

"I don't believe you!"

"Have it your own way, but I'm not staying out here. I'm

coming in!"

Oscar was disgusted. A hysterical old woman, and a stubborn man. Fine company for a self-respecting robot. Laura obviously wasn't thinking or she would realize that Bennett was right. Radio only had a range of about a dozen parsecs, and even subspace radio waves propagated only about two and a half times the speed of light.

So even if there was something cruising within range, it would still take ten years for the message to get there, and as far as he could judge they were much more than a dozen parsecs away from anything familiar. An SOS was like whistling for water on this desert. It might bring it, but the chance was too remote for anything more than statistical significance.

But there was no use in reasoning with a hysterical woman—and less use in reasoning with a stubborn man.

The crawler came rushing toward the ship, and vanished behind a sheet of searing flame from Laura's blaster! The tough alloy of its shell didn't melt, but the machine stopped. Bennett wasn't driving any farther!

"Idiot," Laura said as she recharged the blaster. "He should have known I meant it," she looked at her hands. They were quite steady. "I'd have given him supplies," she muttered defensively. "I just didn't want him on the same ship with me."

She looked out at the stalled crawler, obviously debating whether or not she should go out and inspect the results of her shot. The wind blew stronger, sending a few grains of sand rattling against the hull. She shook her head and turned back toward the interior. There'd be plenty of time tomorrow.

The sun dropped below the horizon, and as it vanished, the heat of the day was abruptly transformed to the cool of evening. And into the coolness came the wind, rushing to fill the vacuum created by the shrinking air mass. In a matter of seconds, the whispering silence was broken, as a howling gale picked up masses of sand and hurled them at the ship!

It was so sudden, so violent, that Laura turned deathly pale and the pounding beat of her suddenly racing heart tapped like tiny hammers in her temples. She fled up the shaft to her level, opened the door of her freshly sanitized cabin, and dropped on her couch, shaking with uncontrollable reaction.

The wind had come too suddenly, a hammer blow that had smashed her taut nerves. With trembling fingers she switched on the cabin lights and turned on the recorder. She wanted sound—noise to drown out the whistling shriek of the wind outside.

The red eye of the pilot light gleamed comfortably at her as the opening chords of the Nine Worlds Symphony crashed from the speakers. The sound filled the cabin, beating against the shriek of the wind and drowning it in a torrent of warmly human music. But only for a moment.

Through the music, ripping in, shrieking counterpoint to the thunder of the orchestration came, the wind. The ship swayed as a howling shriek, amplified by the drumming plates of the hull echoed and reechoed through the ship in endless dissonance. Normality was gone, shattered beyond recall by that hellish blast of sound. Laura screamed, the raw note even louder than the howling din surrounding her. A sly look crept into her eyes. Here was the antidote. All she had to do was scream—and keep on screaming—and keep on screaming,—and—keep—on—

Laura looked vaguely around her. She was lying on the cabin floor. The fainting spell had been just overwrought nerves screaming for release in a body that had absorbed too much physical and mental punishment. She sat up unsteadily, shaking her head from side to side. Outside the din had abated to a steady whistle, and the ship didn't shake nearly so much as it had done in the beginning. She smiled weakly. That had been a whingdinger of a hysterical attack. But that was all over now. Everything was settled and she was all right again.

Stiffly she rose to her feet and made her way to the control room. The vision screen looked out on a scene of utter desolation. The sun must be up for it was light outside—a grayish yellow light obscured by tons of flying sand driven by a rushing wind.

The implications weren't lost on her. She was dead! Dead and buried! Entombed beneath millions of tons of sand!

Oh, not now. Maybe not for another week or month. But in the end it was inevitable. For after all, dunes move, and the one beside the ship had moved perceptibly. Already the lower parts, the main drive and entrance ports were buried. The dune had moved inexorably forward to immobilize the ship. She was trapped.

As she watched the wind died. It was as though some cosmic hand had shut off a giant blower. One moment the sand was rushing through the air, the next it was falling out of Aurum's brazen sky as the sun climbed toward the zenith.

She shrugged. Well, that was that. She could lose without whining. She moved to rise from the pilot's chair—where she was sitting, and a heavy hand pressed her down again. She couldn't see who it was, but those long muscular fingers with the coarse hairs on their backs could belong to only one man on this world—George Bennett!

"Don't move, Mrs. Latham."

Bennett's cold admonition had absolutely no meaning. She couldn't have moved if her life depended on it. He circled the chair. His shirt was off and the pinkish, faintly rippling flesh that covered the left side of his chest marked where the splash of her shot had struck. The flesh was already well on the way to regenerating, and the sight was sickening. His cold eyes inspected her impersonally. There was no anger in them, just a curious remote quality that drove the blood from her face and left her weak and shaking. She had seen that look before.

"Two inches to the right, and I'd still be out there," he said bleakly: "It wasn't a bad shot for a woman."

She stared at him, numb with terror.

"You should have checked to make sure," he said. "Or at least you should have closed the entrance port," he sat gingerly in the copilot's chair, eyeing her with a puzzled look on his face. "But what I can't understand is why you shot me in the first place."

"I was afraid of you," she said dully. "You'd lost your conditioning."

He eyed her coldly, waiting.

"What are you going to do?"

"I don't know," he said with bitter honesty. "I don't go for killing, but there's no sense giving you another chance."

"I wouldn't take it if I had it!" she said shakily. "Last night was enough for a lifetime. I don't think I could go through that again."

"You had quite a party."

"You knew?"

"I was outside your door. I was going to kill you before you started screaming, but I changed my mind."

"Why?"

"I need you. With this bad side, I won't be worth a darn for a week or so, and a week of those sandstorms is going to bury this crate. I need your muscles."

"What can I do?"

"Work. Clean the useful gear out of this ship and help transport it over to the mesa. There's shelter there."

"How? The sandstorm must have buried the crawler."

"I doubt it. I put it on automatic when I came in. It's

probably circling around outside. The sand can't hurt it, but it would have been buried if I had left it motionless. Now let's get moving. We'll start with the food stores first, and don't get any foolish ideas. I'd just as soon burn you as not."

LAURA SLUMPED BESIDE the last crate to be moved. Her body was a living ache of strained muscles and sore joints. It had been killing work to unload everything that Bennett thought he might need, and to lower the gear through the emergency exit to the ground below. Bennett looked down from the hatch at the mound of stores and equipment on the ground. "All right," he called out. "Get that box out. We can't wait all day."

Laura groaned and moved. She was going to feel this day for the rest of her life.

"The crawler isn't going to hold all that stuff and us too," Bennett observed. "You'll have to walk."

"Walk! After all this!"

"You can stay here then," he answered grimly. "I don't need you now."

"I'll walk," she said.

Bennett grinned. "Now, Laura, that's what I call being reasonable."

She looked at him dully. "Who cares?"

"I don't. But I'm glad to see that you've gotten some sense. Now if this short trip across the desert doesn't kill you, you'll be comfortable enough. There's enough room on that mesa for us to never see each other."

"You'd like me to die, wouldn't you?"

"I can't say that it'd cause me any great pain," he admitted. "But still, your company might be preferable to none, I don't know. Anyway, we'll find out if you survive."

"I'll survive," she promised him grimly.

"I don't doubt it," he said. "But before you go I want you

to put on one of the suit liners," he meant the space suit liners—skin tight garments of duralon that fitted closely around wrist and ankles with elastic cuffs. The liner was pocket-less and fitted its wearer like a second skin.

"Why that?"

"First, it's protection of sorts. Second, you won't be able to hide anything under it."

"Cautious lad, aren't you. In that thing I can't even hide myself. It's next door to being stark naked. I'm damned if I will."

"It's your funeral," he said as he swung one leg over the hatch. "But don't try to follow me unless you have that liner on. I'm warning you."

She shrugged. "All right. But I'm going to remember this."

"I don't particularly care whether you do or not."

Oscar thought that this was a fine way to start a long companionship. Between his attitude and hers there was bound to be—the protection ended suddenly in the middle of Oscar's train of thought.

"You turned me off then," Oscar said. "That was inhuman. Turning off my power was virtually the same as killing me."

"I had to," Bennett said. "I didn't know how long we'd be gone and there was no sense in letting you waste power."

Bennett shook his head. His past was no longer a mystery. He had found out what he wanted—and it wasn't too different from what he had deduced. However, Laura certainly wasn't what he thought she'd be. A homicidal neurotic was the last thing he'd have suspected. Quietly he left the control room, ignoring Oscar's protesting squawk that there were still more questions.

CHAPTER TEN

BENNETT ENERGIZED THE antigravity plate on which he had ridden to the bottom of the shaft and rose to the surface of the dune. He entered the crawler and drove slowly back to the mesa where Laura was waiting. How much should he tell her? If he knew her, she'd demand it all, but was he capable of giving it? He'd better let Oscar do it. He realized that the cold facts that the robot would present without emotion would hardly be likely to ease the blow. But it wouldn't be much better if he did it himself. It was a case of being damned if he did and damned if he didn't. He sighed and shook his head.

Laura was waiting for him. "Well," she asked. "Did you find out what you wanted to know?"

"I did, and I didn't."

"What kind of answer is that? What's wrong with you? You're looking strange."

"I suppose so."

"What did you find out?"

"I don't want to talk about it."

"Was it that bad?"

"It wasn't good."

"Did you learn how to fly that ship?"

"Yes. That wasn't hard. I still have the old skills, but I just didn't have the knowledge. About three weeks preflight and I should be able to handle her all right."

"Well, what on earth makes you look as though someone hit you over the head."

"You."

She stood up and faced him. "Now, look, George. I can't

stand any more of this. Either you tell me what happened down there, or I'll go and find out for myself."

He watched her walk across the room with quick impatient steps. He looked at her doubtfully. She was watching him with that familiar speculative look—the look that said in effect that he was going to do what she wanted in the end, so he might as well do it now. Well, he'd tell her— but she wouldn't like it.

Laura looked at him when he had finished. He had been as tactful as he could, but more than once he felt her body stiffen under his hands. But toward the end she had relaxed, even when he told her of the last day aboard the ship.

"She was pretty awful, wasn't she?" Laura asked when he had finished.

"She?"

"Why, Laura Latham, of course. She didn't have very much to live for, did she? It's a good thing that she's dead!"

"Dead?"

"Certainly. In fact, she never happened—not to me at any rate. She's a future I have no part in nor want any part of."

"But my darling. You're Laura Latham!"

"I'm not. I couldn't be. She was something that simply can't happen now. Don't you see, I've nothing in common with her. I never met John Latham. I never married him. I'm twenty-two years old."

He laughed! Subjective to the end! That was a woman for you. She didn't want to know about Laura Latham to find out what she had been, but to find out what she might become! And having learned, she dismissed it as something that simply couldn't exist. Perhaps that was the best way to treat it. After all they both had a new start, were taking a second chance with life—and certainly their lives would be different than they had been before.

Laura was still talking. "Aurum she called it. The Golden

World. It isn't a bad name. I think I like it. It showed that she hadn't lost all love of beauty. There was still something good in her."

The dreaminess left Laura's face and her voice hardened. "But anyway, that doesn't matter. As far as I'm concerned, she never existed."

"Tell that to the immigration lads when I bring you back to Earth and see how far you get," Bennett said. "Your retinal pattern and fingerprints still say you're Laura Latham. You're still the owner of Spaceways and one of the richest women in the Confederation—whatever else you may think you are."

"Then I won't go back. I won't play a part, live a lie. Do you understand? I will not—"

"But you must. I can't leave you here alone."

"Stay here with me then."

"We've gone over this ground before," Bennett said impatiently. "We can't leave a source of knowledge like this untapped. Civilization needs it."

"I'm not interested in Civilization."

"That's not true. You can't help but be interested. You're a part of it—and your good fortune isn't yours alone. It belongs to others as well. Let's face it. When you came here you were a pretty sad specimen if Oscar's telling the truth, and I'm quite sure he is. Now you're pretty wonderful. Would you deny others the right to a second chance?"

"No, but if it means that I'll have to leave this place permanently and become someone I loathe, I'm not going to do it. I don't want power now—at least not that kind. I'm happy here, and I'd just as soon stay that way."

"Nobody's asking you to stay away. But there is going to have to be some sort of machinery set up to make this world available to deserving people in the Confederation. Surely you must realize that. With the money and power you possess back on earth, the process can be speeded up appreciably."

"But George, I can't do it. I just can't. Even if I wanted to I couldn't. If I'm as rich as you claim, I'd be pretty well known, and I simply can't come back looking like a debutante. I'd be a worldwide sensation. And you know what would happen then. People would start asking questions about where I got the rejuvenation, and there'd be all sorts of trouble. By the time it was over, Aurum would be public property with a couple of hundred billion people clamoring to come here. Every world in Civilization would claim this place. We'd have no right at all and our lovely world would be ruined by people who wanted nothing from it but the secret of how to live indefinitely. We're increasing in numbers fast enough now, but if we were all immortal there would be the devil to pay. Civilization isn't ready for that yet."

Bennett started. He hadn't thought of that. Living constantly as a young man, he had forgotten what growing old was like. But it was obvious enough that people grew old—and that they probably hated it. She was right. If word got around that someone had found a way to defeat old age, everyone would be after it. It would probably be worse than the Uranium strike on Halsey that nearly broke the Confederation wide open.

And neither of them would be able to keep the secret. Powerful as Spaceways was, it was not as powerful as the Confederation, and every politician in the Fifty Worlds would be hot on the trail in behalf of themselves and their constituents.

No, Laura was right, he couldn't publicize Aurum. Its benefits would have to be conferred secretly on those who could use them intelligently. There would have to be some sort of screening, and the technology here would have to be released slowly, over enough time for Civilization to absorb its impact. In time perhaps even immortality could be given to everyone. But Laura had proposed problems he hadn't yet considered—and they were real.

To throw a concept of paradise in the face of the galaxy would do precisely that which he wished to prevent. It would create tensions, wars, and anarchy until someone recognized the only way to cut the Gordian knot. And then Aurum would vanish forever in the flare of a phoenix explosion. Common sense told him that this was the only solution if the word got around. So the word couldn't get around—at least not promiscuously—and Laura couldn't go back to Civilization—at least not as Laura Latham.

She looked at him expectantly. Obviously he was supposed to say something, and when he did not, she finally spoke. "There's a solution to this, you know.'"

"There is?"

"Certainly. It's obvious that we'll have to select the people who will come here. And it's equally obvious that we'll have to use Spaceways' personnel department to do that—at least in the early stages. I don't remember anything about Spaceways, but if that company is like any other company they're bound to have a very efficient personnel procurement and allocation section."

"The have."

"Well, then as I see it the problem all revolves around me. I own Spaceways, but I can't take control because I've regressed some forty years. But you've only gone back ten. I'll bet you hardly look any different than you did, and the little changes could be handled with a bit of makeup. Since I was in Video, I know enough about that to make you look old enough to avoid suspicion. Besides, who'd remember a pilot?"

"Lots of people."

"Possibly. But certainly no one of great importance."

Bennett nodded. "But then you want me to do the work?"

"Better than that. I want you to take over Spaceways!"

"You can't mean that!"

"But I do! Since Laura Latham is dead, she'll have to remain that way. I don't think it'd be improper if she left a will leaving everything to you for the tender care you gave her during her last weeks of life. A holographic will stands up in any court, and I don't think my handwriting has changed too much over the years. If it has my fingerprints, it should be a satisfactory signature. I'll bet with Oscar's help we can make it legal enough."

"That brings up another problem," Bennett muttered; "What are we going to do with Oscar?"

"Erase him, of course."

"But you can't erase a ship's computer."

"I'll be willing to bet," Laura said, "that if I was as awful as you've made me believe, I'd have some way to bollix Oscar. If I owned that ship, I owned a key to that robot. It would be out of character if I didn't. If I was a stinker—and I'm sure I was a good one—the possibility of an incriminating record was something I wouldn't have chanced to let out of my hands."

"All right, granting that—and I'll admit it's a good possibility—what about me doublecrossing you and going off with all that money of yours."

She smiled. "I know you better than that, but if you tried, I could always come to life."

"I could kill you."

"No, you couldn't. You're not a criminal type. If you were, I wouldn't be here after I tried to shoot you."

He grinned. "Whatever may have happened to your outlook you still haven't lost your brain. Well, then, now that we've decided to kill Laura Latham off, let's polish the details. I'll take the plan to Collie and have her go over it and iron out the flaws."

"That seems sensible enough."

"Now about the ship. I'll get the meks on it and have her patched up as good as new."

"Not that good. It'd be suspicious. No more than could be done by one man working without help for four years."

"I know, I didn't mean quite what I said. I'll repair the tanks, patch the holes, and restore the steering jets, but I won't have the meks do a finished job. I'll leave it crude— but workable."

She shrugged. "That's your problem. As far as mechanics are concerned I'll sit it out. But I'm coming with you, of course. We'll have to figure out some way to get me to Earth without rousing too much suspicion, but you're going to need me on the sidelines if things get tough. But I'm sure you'll pull through all right. I have confidence in you."

"That's not confidence…that's plain foolishness. But if it works, we have it made."

"It'll work all right. No one will possibly question us after Collie works the plan over. It'll be airtight. And once we get settled you can start organizing Altruism Incorporated."

"Huh?" Bennett looked blank.

"Your noble plans for the betterment of humanity. If you're smart, you'll incorporate."

"Why?"

"It's obvious," Laura replied. "A corporation is the only thing in our civilization that has a personality and lives forever. If we worked in person, a few decades would give away our secret, but under the cover of a corporate body we could move freely. Since you're so eager to give everything we have away, let's go about it sensibly. A corporation is expected to be ageless. Look at General Electronics. It can trace its life clear back to the General Electric Corporation of the Dark Ages. And we'll need something with a life span at least that long to accomplish our purposes."

"That's taking a long view of it."

"That's the only view we can take. Actually, that'll be our only advantage, and we must have it to control the one thing that's important. With the power of granting eternal youth we can do anything. Ultimately we'll have every outstanding scientist and philosopher in the galaxy in our organization, and with them on our team, we'll never be touched. In the end we'll control the Confederation."

"But I don't want that."

"You can't avoid it. It's inevitable. It's the only way we can keep what we have unless we stay here forever and say nothing. If we're going to be altruistic, we'll have to do it on a sound business basis, within the laws of Civilization."

Bennett chuckled. "I see how you become a power. You had the ability all along."

"I don't want this—not really," she said. "And I think we should make Collie chairman of the board. Her brain is better than either of ours, and her attitude is much better. I'm selfish, and you're foolish. But she's been conditioned to service, and she won't let us down."

"Collie's going to like it," he said. "It'll give her something to do that'll make her use her powers. And in the meantime," he ruffled her hair with one big hand, "I think we'd better keep our feet on the ground and let her work out the details. There's no sense in having a superior mind available and not use it."

Laura sighed and settled herself in his lap. "That's the first thing you've said that has the elements of real sense."

"I've been saving Civilization," he grinned. "There hasn't been time to be sensible."

"There's all the time in the world. There's years ahead of

us, and I'm going to have my share of them."

Bennett smiled at her. "You're a very demanding woman," he said.

"I know it," she replied complacently, "but I never demand what I can't get," she twisted in his arms and kissed him full on the mouth.

"You're incorrigible!" Bennett chuckled.

"It's just animal spirits," she said demurely. "Let Collie run the altruism. It's a proper job for her. And in the meantime I'll run you. At least, part of the time."

THE END

If you've enjoyed this book, you will not want to miss these terrific titles…

ARMCHAIR SCI-FI & HORROR DOUBLE NOVELS, $12.95 each

D-11   **PERIL OF THE STARMEN** by Kris Neville
        THE FORGOTTEN PLANET by Murray Leinster

D-12   **THE STAR LORD** by Boyd Ellanby
        CAPTIVES OF THE FLAME by Samuel R. Delaney

D-13   **MEN OF THE MORNING STAR** by Edmund Hamilton
        PLANET FOR PLUNDER by Hal Clement and Sam Merwin, Jr.

D-14   **ICE CITY OF THE GORGON** by Chester S. Geier and Richard S. Shaver
        WHEN THE WORLD TOTTERED by Lester Del Rey

D-15   **WORLDS WITHOUT END** by Clifford D. Simak
        THE LAVENDER VINE OF DEATH by Don Wilcox

D-16   **SHADOW ON THE MOON** by Joe Gibson
        ARMAGEDDON EARTH by Geoff St. Reynard

D-17   **THE GIRL WHO LOVED DEATH** by Paul W. Fairman
        SLAVE PLANET by Laurence M. Janifer

D-18   **SECOND CHANCE** by J. F. Bone
        MISSION TO A DISTANT STAR by Frank Belknap Long

D-19   **THE SYNDIC** by C. M. Kornbluth
        FLIGHT TO FOREVER by Poul Anderson

D-20   **SOMEWHERE I'LL FIND YOU** by Milton Lesser
        THE TIME ARMADA by Fox B. Holden

ARMCHAIR SCIENCE FICTION CLASSICS, $12.95 each

C-3   **INTO PLUTONIAN DEPTHS**
        by Stanton A. Coblentz

C-4   **CORPUS EARTHLING**
        by Louis Charbonneau

C-5   **THE TIME DISSOLVER**
        by Jerry Sohl

C-6   **WEST OF THE SUN**
        by Edgar Pangborn

ARMCHAIR SCIENCE FICTION & HORROR GEMS SERIES, $12.95 each

G-1   **SCIENCE FICTION GEMS, Vol. One**
        Isaac Asimov and others

G-2   **HORROR GEMS, Vol. One**
        Carl Jacobi and others

THE "FRIENDLY" INVASION OF EARTH

When the aliens first appeared on planet Earth, it obviously caused quite a stir. The fanfare was accompanied by a good many overtures of friendship and goodwill on the part of the aliens. Everything seemed very palsy-walsy. And yet, to show mankind the true depth of the enormous power they possessed, the aliens made the stark decision to blow an island off the map one sunny afternoon in the South Pacific. It was just to let mankind know exactly who they were dealing with. But what did the aliens, known as "the Scorpions," really want? What was the well-guarded secret of the disabled Scorpion spaceship that was tucked away in the lonely backwoods of rural Vermont? It was up to a keen political investigator to find out why, but he soon found himself knee deep in the wildest alien conspiracy imaginable…

CAST OF CHARACTERS

JIM LAWRENCE
After years as a savvy political correspondent, he found himself investigating strange alien activities—right in his own hometown.

RUTH FRASER
When she stole a bracelet from a department store she never dreamed anyone would rescue her—let alone an alien being!

D'Qy aka "DUKE"
A man from another world—a "Scorpion." He was the linchpin in a wild alien scheme that might spell doom for many on Earth.

HARVEY JORDAN
He was the Bureau chief, and he handpicked Lawrence to crack an alien plot that, unfortunately, nobody knew anything about.

GILLINGS
This gaunt, elderly man was found wandering aimlessly about in the local marshes, the first apparent victim of alien aggression.

MARK WHITSUN
A friendly fellow—an antique dealer, but what was his ominous connection to the disabled alien spaceship that lay in the woods?

DR. CRAWFORD
The first human attacked by a Scorpion was left in a state of near insanity. It was up to this psychiatrist to unlock his mind.

MISSION TO A DISTANT STAR

By
FRANK BELKNAP LONG

ARMCHAIR FICTION
PO Box 4369, Medford, Oregon   97501-0168

*For more information about Armchair Books and products, visit our
website at…*

www.armchairfiction.com

Or email us at…

armchairfiction@yahoo.com

PROLOGUE

THERE WAS A strange, unnatural, almost frightening silence in the great hall as the tall visitor arose to speak. His voice was calm and assured, his manner completely relaxed. He made no attempt to be oratorical but spoke with measured accents, as if he were addressing an assemblage of old and trusted friends. But there was something about his grave and thoughtful countenance that commanded instant respect.

The United Nations were in full, plenary session, summoned by an emergency far transcending in gravity the most critical of international crises, and there was no clamor on the part of anyone to take the floor in defense of national interests and national rights.

The tall figure said, "You have asked for proof that we are a responsible and enlightened race. There can be no wisdom without strength, no true enlightenment unless the power to work immense harm exists and is deliberately renounced. Violence is in itself the greatest of all crimes against intelligence everywhere in space.

"We have come to Earth on a scientific mission solely, just as you will someday travel to the stars to—if you will permit me I should like to quote from one of your greatest poets. 'To follow knowledge like a shining star beyond the utmost bounds of human thought.'

"We ask only complete freedom...your friendship, trust and understanding for as long as we shall choose to remain.

"We abhor violence in any form. But since you feel that a demonstration is called for—a demonstration you shall have. Select an island—any island—well outside your ocean trade routes. Be prepared to observe, at a safe distance, the power that we shall unleash. Set a time, a date. That is all we ask of you."

For a moment silence returned to the great hall. Then the Director General arose and said slowly, as if carefully weighing each word, "There is no need for us to put your proposal to a vote. We accept it, unconditionally."

Two weeks later a dozen auxiliary naval cruisers under United Nations mandate stood several miles to leeward of a small coral island in the South Pacific, its precise location veiled in secrecy. Thin shafts of sunlight slanted down over the palm trees through a rift in the gray overcast and a gentle breeze sent small waves rolling up a pebble-strewn beach.

Suddenly high above the island a long, cylindrical shape emerged from the clouds and encircled the palm-fringed atoll twice.

For an instant the Scorpion spaceship seemed to shudder along its entire length. Then a blinding burst of incandescence came from it, sweeping outward and downward until the entire island was enveloped in a bright, steady glow.

When the glow vanished the island was gone.

CHAPTER ONE

THE GAUNT MAN was running. His footsteps echoed hollowly on weed-grown stretches of sunken masonry, and his breath came in long, wheezing gasps. He was running across a lakeside pier, his hands pressed to his face as if to shut out some intolerable sight. The pier was abandoned, old, crumbling at its base.

The fleeing man was old, too. His long white hair and beard streamed in the wind, and there was a stiffness, a crookedness, in the slope of his shoulders as a spasm of terror caused him to swing, abruptly about, and lower his hands for the barest instant—a figure of madness poised for a leap.

He turned and ran on again for a few paces. Then he was at the edge of the pier and he *did* leap—straight out from the side of the pier with a scream that echoed loudly through the night. He landed on his feet in a tangled morass of weeds and marsh grass and went floundering onward, the breath whoosing from his lungs, his blue dungarees gleaming wetly in the moonlight.

He continued his headlong flight, sinking almost knee-deep in mud at times, but defying the impediments in his path—a rotting log which he straddled, a clump of cat-a'-nine-tails which he beat down with his hands, clawing aside the long stalks, fighting his way clear.

He was still within sight of the pier when the moon passed behind a cloud, and from the depths of the marsh a giant bullfrog set up a doleful croaking. It was joined by others of its kind—a chorus of croaking from long-legged male animals almost manlike in aspect.

Manlike, too, perhaps, in the awareness of peril that seems at times to spread throughout the whole of animate nature in an engulfing wave, breaking down and dissolving the barriers between man and the lower animals in the blinking of an eye—an eye frozen with terror, paralyzed in its socket, white and motionless in the still night.

A COMPLETE SCIENCE FICTION NOVEL

Mission to a Distant Star

by FRANK BELKNAP LONG

Only—the night wasn't still. Other voices joined the chorus. From the deep woods lining the shore a great horned owl hooted, a red squirrel started chattering, and a heron went flapping skyward. A cricket sound seemed to rise above the din, but it could just as easily have been the ringing in the gaunt man's own ears as, in a desperately frenzied state now, blind with panic, he found himself bogged down.

He began to moan, to mutter aloud to himself. "Went too near their ship. They must have just wanted to—scare me away. That's it, sure. That *must* be it. Take it easy now. How do you know they're still after you?"

Sweat oozed out under his armpits, chilling his back and groin, mingling with the silt-wetness of his gray flannel shirt.

"Could have been—a man like me. Not even a Scorpion. Just glided toward me. Didn't run—just glided. But I could have been mistaken about that. Suit, shirt, hat—he was dressed ordinarily enough. If it hadn't been for his face—by heavens, his face! If ever there was death in a single glance. And that weapon—" A look of horror came into the old man's eyes.

"Nothing I can do. Can't get away—not if they're really after me. Scorpions never make an unfriendly move—never anything so far to make us afraid of them. Seems like they was always telling us: 'We'll go away if you like, never come back. If that's what you really want, just say so.' "

"Why couldn't we have just said so? What was it stopped our tongues, made us afraid to speak our minds? Afraid? There was no fear. I wasn't afraid. Talked to dozens of them. That one at the hotel Duke. If he was a man you'd say he was—a nice guy. An all right guy. And Scorpions *are* men, in a way—no different from us outwardly.

"Maybe, though, it was fear where it counts most—high up. Not only the Big Brass in Washington, but the Big Brass all over Earth. Hydrogen bomb fear—only a thousand times worse. The Scorpion spaceships. Sure, that's probably it."

The gaunt man raised his eyes. The dawn was just breaking above the trees by the shore and suddenly as he stared a golden-crested bird—invisible to him—burst into song. And almost at the same instant an incredible thing happened.

All of the fear went out of the gaunt man's eyes. He leaned back with a sigh and let the beauty and the freshness of the just-beginning dawn take complete possession of him. He could no longer remember why he had allowed himself to become frightened—could not even recall his flight across the wharf, his desperate leap, his mounting terror as the marsh grew constantly more threatening, and the blind panic which had finally come upon him. Concerning all of these things—he could remember nothing.

He forgot how it felt to be old, remembering only a song played on piano keys by fingers that would never grow cold in death, and white sea-cliffs in the dawn, with gulls wheeling and dipping above the shining tides and the trade winds tossing free.

Miraculously joyful thoughts, thoughts that death could not touch, could not hope to wound. Like high, imperishable galleons they sailed across the calm waters of his mind, casting their shadows on hills where men and women, lithe-limbed and untouched by sorrow, gathered purple grapes.

And when he groped backwards in his mind for a more complete understanding he discovered to his astonishment that everything that had gone before was enveloped in complete darkness.

CHAPTER TWO

The magnificence of the corridor that led to the Bureau Chief's office never failed to awe Jim Lawrence. There was something hushed and resplendent about it, like a big, Fifth Avenue jewelry store after closing hours, with the clerks tabulating the day's receipts, and the diamonds sparkling under glass.

It was ridiculous for Jim Lawrence to feel apprehensive, for his job even permitted him to feel important. He was one of the ablest political correspondents in Washington. He could walk right up and talk to the President, if he felt so inclined—just a simple phone call would get him past the Secret Service barriers. Yet—

Jim Lawrence was remembering: nothing on Earth was securely entrenched, solid, massive, or ever would be again. He was no longer Jim Lawrence, expert news gatherer; he was a member of the human race and as such, a tragically divided, inwardly tormented man at the mercy of the *Great Change*. His lips tightened, and he quickened his step.

A line from a very great poet flashed across his mind. "No man is an island, entire in himself." At one time he'd have scoffed at the suggestion that he couldn't build walls around his own ego high and broad and impregnable enough to make him something of an island, at least.

But now he knew better. Just thinking about the *Great Change* now, just remembering it, drove the blood in torrents from his heart.

He knocked gently, then halted with his hand on the door of the Chief's office, feeling as if someone were threatening his life, his normally handsome face set in haggard lines. How could he have forgotten, even for an instant, the coming of the Scorpions?

True, the Scorpion ships nestled quietly enough in pleasant green valleys all over the Earth. And the Scorpions hadn't committed a single hostile act. They were friendly people—almost too friendly—and it was difficult not to like them.

But the fact remained that the Scorpions were everywhere the conquerors, the overlords—no matter how soft and considerate their tread. Man now existed on his own planet by sufferance only and that fact alone could kill. In a thousand insidious ways it could diminish the human race and reduce the human individual to a pawn.

How far in the past it all seemed now—the beginning, the first sighting of the Scorpion ships in the new, 400-inch reflecting telescope on Mount Palomar. How far away still seemed the Star Antares, blazing in solitary splendor in the night sky—when men still had the courage to stare skyward—the seventeenth brightest star in the sky, with a diameter almost five hundred times that of the Sun.

Antares in the Constellation Scorpius—eighth constellation in the Zodiac, a Scorpion-shaped spiral of fire weaving down the sky. How far in the past it seemed, that beginning, that first sighting. An eternity had passed, surely—an eternity of seven long years. Seven years, a lifetime of shock, bewilderment, slow acceptance as the Scorpion ships took up their stations on Earth. A seven-year lifetime of bowing to the inevitable, a lifetime of change.

Someone was talking so loudly in the Chief's office he could hear the man's voice through the door and that snapped him out of his momentary trance. Lawrence turned the knob, threw open the door and walked into the office feeling suddenly almost normal again.

The Chief was sitting at his desk shuffling through some papers. He said without looking up, "Shut the door, Jim."

Lawrence nodded, and started to swing about. Then he

saw that there were two other men in the office and that the door was being shut for him. One of the two was a calm, efficient-looking man in a gray business suit and he had leapt up instantly to close the door before Lawrence could turn back to it.

The second man was very old and very bent. He had snow-white hair and a long beard and looked—well, close to eighty. He sat in a straight-backed chair a little to the right of the door and in his eyes was a strained and watchful look that gave Jim Lawrence a jolt.

His rigidity, his outward composure, were quite obviously only skin-deep. Muscle-deep at most, and Lawrence got the impression that his nervous control was in such an advanced stage of deterioration that he might at any moment leap from the chair with a wild shriek.

The Chief raised his eyes then, and looked at Lawrence and said, "Draw up a chair, Jim. We've got something important to discuss."

The man in the gray business suit nodded. "We're in trouble, Mr. Lawrence. We're hoping that you can help us. I'm Dr. Crawford, Psychiatric Division, U.S.I."

Lawrence acknowledged the self-introduction with a quick, firm handshake. He wondered for a moment why the Chief was letting the Intelligence officer do the talking, and then decided that he was jumping to a premature conclusion. Bureau Chief Harvey Jordan believed in delegating authority to specialists in moments of crisis as firmly as the next man, but he had little inclination to play second fiddle to anyone in his own office.

He said, "I'll do the explaining, John, if you don't mind."

Dr. Crawford grunted and sat down.

The Chief shifted around impatiently in his chair, regarding Lawrence with a look of somber appeal. "I must ask you not to interrupt me, Jim—until I'm through. You're a highly intelligent man and not likely to dismiss as bewildering and incomprehensible a danger that could kill us all."

Lawrence edged his chair a little closer to the Chief's desk. He knew from experience that Jordan was not an alarmist. If anything, the Chief erred by showing no inclination to succumb to bleak despair when he contemplated the Scorpion threat.

The Chief started to speak again, then stopped. The old man had half-risen from his chair and was muttering audibly. The words that poured from his shaking lips startled and disturbed Lawrence, so shocking were they in their irrelevancy.

"It was a glory, I tell you...a glory. I was just sitting there looking up at the trees when there was no fear at all in me...I can't remember why...no need to remember, don't want to remember. Just the glory."

The old man's talk had been wild enough, in sober truth, but for a moment at least there was no hostility in his stare. Then suddenly he was on his feet, his face convulsed with a fury so intense that it gave him the aspect of a madman.

"You tried—to make me remember! You had no right. You tried to bring it all back. I can't remember what I told you. But it was an agony. It was like dying—over and over."

"Be quiet, Gillings," Crawford pleaded. "Be quiet, man. We need your help. You haven't been harmed in any way. I brought you here because I wanted you to meet and talk with Mr. Lawrence as you are. We're all your friends."

He turned suddenly and gestured toward Lawrence, and Jim's jaw fell open at his next words. "This man is from your own home town, Gillings. Do you understand? Your own village—Quarry Hill—in Vermont."

Lawrence remembered him then. Through the blue haze of a very great distance—his own adolescence—the memory of a younger Gillings returned, so sharply and distinctly that the man himself seemed to come striding toward him along a pier. The younger Gillings had been a carpenter with a small farm of his own and had later turned to renting rowboats and canoes to fishermen at the lake.

Quite a character he had been, and Lawrence could remember the man's friendliness and his wit, and even the tattoo marks on his arm—two big blue-and-yellow dragons and an arrow-pierced heart.

There were seamen in Vermont now who had scorpions tattooed on their arms—only a few, fortunately, and they were callow young fools too stupid to realize that they had turned themselves into symbolic robot-slaves. Still—

The old man had slumped despairfully forward in his chair, his hands on his knees, his gaunt angularity very much in evidence but lending him no strength.

"We're wasting a great deal of valuable time," Dr. Crawford said quietly. "I've got to get Gillings back to the hospital and...well, suppose you let *me* tell Jim Lawrence about Gillings, and the Scorpion Ship."

To Lawrence's amazement, Harvey Jordan acquiesced. He seemed unhappy about it and had gone a little pale, but all he said was, "All right, go ahead."

"Gillings was in a state of absolute amnesia," Crawford said. "Couldn't remember why he had gone into the marsh, couldn't remember a thing. He was brought to us simply because—well, there are twenty-seven Scorpion ships in all and only one was wrecked beyond repair. I mean, beyond repair from our point of view. I've no doubt that the Scorpions will eventually repair it. The ships in England, France, Germany and the Soviet Union could take off tomorrow, but one of the ships that landed in America seems to be permanently berthed here."

"I know," Jim Lawrence said. "I also know that it put my

native town quite definitely on the map, and that Quarry Hill has made a tourist attraction of what's left of it. With the cooperation of the Scorpions, of course. Apparently they want to make their grounded starship look impressive to the natives."

"There's no need for them to make it look impressive," Crawford said. "It would be impressive if it contained only one battered navigational instrument, half a rocket-tube and a few skeleton props. Actually, it's nine-tenths intact. Harvey will tell you after I've taken Gillings back to the hospital just why that ship has become so important to us and what you can do to help. We're concerned right now with what happened to Gillings—and just why he was flown to Washington so fast."

"Well, why was he?" Lawrence asked.

"Simply because he was found dazed and wandering helplessly through a swamp a half-mile from that Scorpion ship. I have seldom seen a case of amnesia so complete and—yes, terrifying. It's one thing to have a few years blotted out—quite another not to be able to remember a single place, name, face in your past from infancy onward."

Lawrence looked concernedly at Gillings, but the man seemed completely unaware of what was being said.

"It was no ordinary case of amnesia," Crawford went on. "There was no *educational* blackout. By that I mean that he remembers everything he learned at school-like grammar and history. His speech is unimpaired. All right. You'd think if he could remember his history lessons at school he could remember the face of his teacher, his own name. Well, he can't remember a single thing that ever happened to him personally. His mind has become a kind of selective sieve. The educational process has seeped through, but the rest has been blacked out. And of course the human mind just isn't made that way."

"It's impossible—but it happened," Lawrence said. "Is that what you're trying to say?"

"It's what I *am* saying. I spoke of a sieve. It's more as if some tremendous mechanical intelligence—I'm thinking of a giant computer or cybernetic brain a million times as complex as the ones we're familiar with—as if some tremendous intelligence had gotten inside his mind and was carefully guarding it, pruning away the personality circuits, to prevent any *self*-memories from taking command."

Lawrence nodded. "I think then your first problem would be to convince him that you were his friend." He looked at the old man as he spoke, but Gillings seemed completely lost in his own thoughts.

"We did our best in that respect," Crawford said, "but he resented the slightest probing. It was as if—well, as if we were desecrating some inner glory that was more precious to him than awareness of self.

"We tried the so-called 'truth serum' drugs—sodium amytal, sodium nembutal and finally, sodium pentothal. Of the three, sodium pentothal is the most powerful, but it is also the most unpredictable. It simply made him retreat more completely into himself. And actually, he had no self to retreat into—in the customarily accepted sense. Just—the glory."

"But you didn't stop with the drugs," the Chief said, emerging rather abruptly. "You tried hypnosis."

Crawford nodded. "We did and—miracle of miracles—it worked. Any reasonably unbiased psychologist will tell you that hypnosis is the most unpredictable technique of all. Gillings may or may not be an hysteric in a strict sense. But a terrible, mind-numbing fright is usually at the root of an hysterical neurosis with its almost inconceivable phobias. We were groping, understand, but we did have a pretty strong hunch that Gillings had been frightened in some terrible way. We gambled on that and it paid off."

The Chief started to speak again, but Crawford silenced him with an impatient gesture. "Suppose we put it this way. You can't force a man under hypnosis to do anything he doesn't really want to do, anything that goes violently against his basic conditioning. But somewhere, deep down in Gillings' mind, he *wanted* to remember, *wanted* to talk. There was some unnatural influence holding him back; something, we think, that had been artificially introduced into his mind. We'll call it the 'glory' block—the personality blackout.

"You see, the personality hookups—or neural synapses, if you want to be technical—hadn't been totally obliterated. The giant computer I used as a far from exact illustration had gotten inside his mind, all right. It had done some short-circuiting, but apparently wasn't quite complex and efficient enough to bring about a complete amputation.

"In fact, the memories we wanted to activate were probably all still very much alive—just playing possum. Under hypnosis part of his mind—the victimized part—resisted, even fought us violently. But another part yielded and wanted to *talk*. Part of his mind remembered."

"What—did he remember?" Lawrence asked, aware of a chill prickling at the base of his scalp.

"He remembered the wrecked Scorpion spaceship. Everything that happened to him when he saw a strange light playing over it and went close to investigate."

Lawrence turned quickly, staring in concern at the old man. But Gillings' face was now a complete blank. If Crawford's forthright statement had impinged on his consciousness in any way, he gave no sign.

As if aware of Lawrence's thoughts, Crawford said, "Don't worry. He doesn't know what we're talking about. His outward orientation is almost hallucinatory, as I've told you.

If anything sets him off it will come from within himself. Naturally, I'll feel relieved when he's safely back at the hospital. But now suppose we talk about what he saw. He saw something—pretty ghastly."

The Chief said, "Let me tell him...Jim, when he went close to the Scorpion ship a Scorpion—or a man—came out of the ship with a very strange weapon in his hand. It was a kind of—well, a machine-pistol, with a very long barrel. We've never seen a Scorpion weapon, remember—but what they did to that South Pacific Island and their technological achievements in all other respects would make their possession of many powerful small weapons a certainty.

"But Gillings was the first man ever to actually see a Scorpion weapon. That, in and of itself, gave him a jolt. There was something about that long, pistol-like gun that held him entranced for a minute. Then he began to shake. A *feeling* came upon him he couldn't throw off—a feeling of *deadliness.*"

"His terror when he described it was unnerving to watch," Crawford interposed, leaning sharply forward in his chair. "He turned deathly pale, shook and thrashed about. Sweat came out on his forehead. It completely demoralized him."

"That isn't all, Jim," Jordan said. "The figure itself was even more terrifying. It moved toward him in a kind of snakelike glide. For a moment it seemed almost to rise from the ground, to be spread-eagled against empty air. Then it came nearer and he saw its face. You'd better describe it, John."

Crawford smiled thinly. "I can describe it calmly only because I wasn't standing there looking at it. If I'd been in Gillings shoes I doubt if I could have described it at all, even under hypnosis. As near as I can judge from what Gillings told us, it was a Scorpion face. You know how their features differ from ours—much higher cheekbones, as a rule, and a comeliness that puts us in the shade."

"I know," Lawrence said.

"Well, the comeliness was there structurally. But the expression distorted it. Rage. A cold, merciless rage that seemed to seep into Gillings' bones, chilling him to the core. Or perhaps—it wasn't rage. From what Gillings said we can't be completely sure. It could have been—simply a cold determination *not to be interfered with.*"

"Whatever it was, it frightened him enough to administer a psychic trauma," the Chief said. "He screamed in terror and ran, his only thought to escape. Minute by minute the terror kept getting worse. It was so bad that—well, it might in and of itself have given him amnesia."

"But it didn't," Crawford interrupted quickly. "Something else caused the mental blackout. He was bogged down, deep in the marsh, when it happened. Quite suddenly—he couldn't remember what had caused him to flee from the wreck in blind, unreasoning terror. He couldn't even remember where he was, how he had clawed and fought his way deep into the marsh. A great peace came upon him, a calmness, majestic and beautiful—like a dream of paradise. And when they found him—he was still like that."

CHAPTER THREE

GILLINGS STILL sat in his chair, passively listening, but saying nothing. His utter calmness, his impassivity, right up to the instant when Crawford stopped speaking was what made his violent outburst seem so unnatural.

He made straight for Crawford, his heavily veined, claw-like hands reaching out for the startled medical officer's throat. Crawford upset his chair in a frantic effort to escape from the maniacal fury he saw in the old man's eyes. He went back so far he collided with the wall and was unable to regain his equilibrium fast enough.

Abruptly Gillings was upon him, clutching his throat in a strangling grip, squeezing, refusing to let go.

"You had no right to make me remember," he muttered, his voice guttural, harsh, as if each syllable had been wrenched from him by an inner agony that could no longer be endured. You've never been there yourself—so you don't know."

The old man's thumbs were pressing cruelly into the soft flesh above Crawford's windpipe when Jim Lawrence got to him, gripping, him relentlessly by the elbows, permitting Crawford to break free.

Lawrence struck him then, sharply on the jaw, hating to do it, but knowing that it was sensible, necessary, wise—that the old man must be dropped to the floor as quickly as possible, if only to prevent him from injuring himself.

But Gillings didn't drop to the floor. He reeled a little and shook his head but he didn't go down. Instead he swung about and faced Lawrence and started fighting back, furiously, crazily, not seeming to care where his blows landed. He scratched, kicked, beat with his fists on Lawrence's chest, thrust upwards with his elbows, dodged and weaved about.

It was the kind of struggle that would have seemed grotesque, almost farcical on the screen, but to Jim Lawrence it was deadly dangerous. Superior strength, youth even, is seldom a match for a maniac, no matter how advanced his age.

The old man was fighting silently now, making no sound at all. A strange feeling had settled over Lawrence's mind— half inertia, half panic. The whole ghastly situation seemed a little unreal. Why should Gillings put up so fierce a resistance when he had sat impassive for so long? What word, inflexion, disembodied thought had set him off?

Jim Lawrence had no way of knowing that it was a *presence* that had set Gillings off. The presence was not there in the room with them, he couldn't see it or hear it yet and so his utter incomprehension made sense.

It made perhaps more sense to the Scorpion who at that moment emerged from the elevator at the end of the corridor and advanced with unhurried steps toward the office, but Lawrence had no way of knowing that either, no opportunity even to speculate about it. Only gradually did he become aware that he was no longer in danger, that both Jordan and Crawford were advancing on Gillings with a grim confidence in their eyes which left no doubt as to their ability to subdue him.

There were perhaps ten seconds more of unreason in the saddle, of a madman's futile struggles to remain destructively at large. Then Gillings was gripped by strong arms and held in a rigid straitjacket of bone and sinew that permitted him no freedom of movement at all.

"I'll need assistance in getting him back to the hospital now," Crawford said, his voice so decisive and professional that it grated on Lawrence and made him angry.

"Let up on him a little, can't you?" he protested. "You're hurting him."

Crawford shook his head. "No. I'm not hurting him at all. Let me handle this, please. It's a necessary part of my job."

For what could only have been the fraction of a minute a heavy silence brooded in the room, while the Chief returned to his desk. He had picked up the phone and was just starting to dial the hospital when the door opened and the Scorpion stepped into the room.

The Scorpion looked surprised. His heavy eyelids lifted slightly and he said with the slight, peculiar accent that is inseparable from the Scorpion tongue, "I beg your pardon. I'm afraid I'm in the wrong office. I wonder if you could direct me to—"

He paused, as if seeing Gillings for the first time—taking in at a single glance the old man's rigidly straining body and the strong, firm hands that held him pinioned in an iron clasp.

"Why," he said, "something pretty serious seems to have taken place here. Can I be of any help?"

Crawford made no reply. He simply stared, a look of stunned incredulity in his eyes. Quite obviously the Scorpion's unexpected appearance at precisely that moment had unnerved him. And though his brain worked fast and he fought inwardly to fortify himself against the shock and to keep stark fear at bay, fear was there, in a darkly shuttered part of his mind.

It was no good telling himself that Scorpions frequently visited Washington—visited every Government building, walked in and out of the echoing corridors with as much freedom and independence as the average American citizen enjoyed. It was their privilege, their right. It had been bestowed upon them as a privilege and a right by the American public at the polls, confirmed by an act of Congress and signed into law by the President.

A Scorpion, appearing suddenly in the doorway of a Government office, would ordinarily have been too normal and natural a sight to evoke the slightest alarm. In all likelihood this one had come to consult a vacation folder put out by the Department—an ordinary news information service available to anyone—or to question a meteorologist about weather predictions for a New England state.

What reason could Lawrence advance for this particular Scorpion's arrival? What reason beyond the fact that he had appeared at the precise moment of a tragic struggle between a mentally unbalanced old man and three Government employees in a highly agitated state'?

Certainly there was nothing unusual about the Scorpion's aspect or attire. He wore a handsomely tailored gray business suit and a gray knitted tie, for Scorpions liked to dress conservatively when they abandoned the attire natural to them for garments that they seemed able to wear with a more than terrestrial dignity and grace. There were never any bulges, any ill-fitting shoulder pleats, despite their muscular build and the boniness of their broad, firm-fleshed chests. On a Scorpion even a modestly priced suit would have looked good.

The Scorpion's eyes were bland and green-yellow and they gleamed with sympathetic concern as he waited for

Crawford's reply. They shifted once to Lawrence and then back again to Crawford. But their owner showed no excitement as a man might have done on coming unexpectedly upon a scene of unusual violence and finding the participants incapable of speech, frozen in their tracks, and by their looks and gestures seeming to accuse him of being a monster, a fiend…

Crawford found his voice at last. "This is a Government matter," he said. "It concerns nobody but these three gentlemen and myself."

"I'm truly sorry," the Scorpion said. "It was not my intention to intrude. As you are acting as agents of the Government there must naturally be many ramifications involved here about which I have no right to inquire. All of them," he added seriously, "entirely creditable to you. Of that I am sure."

He nodded, inclined his shoulders slightly, and turned back toward the door through which he had so unexpectedly stepped an eternity ago. At least, it seemed that long to Lawrence and in all probability to Crawford, whose face had turned as white as the piled-up documents on the Chief's desk. As for Jordan himself, he seemed incapable of speech, too appalled and shaken to do more than nod.

The Scorpion smiled slightly in return and, the great muscles of his shoulders seeming to ripple a little under his coat, went out of the door without a backward glance. His footsteps receding down the corridor could be heard clearly for eight or ten seconds.

There ensued a silence. It was not entirely absolute, however, for it was broken at intervals by Gillings' harsh breathing. Then, all at once, the breathing stopped.

From the instant of the Scorpion's shockingly-timed appearance to his unnervingly courteous departure neither Lawrence nor Crawford had paid much attention to Gillings.

Beyond retaining his grip upon the man, Crawford had ignored him completely.

Had he not done so he would have noticed the unnatural pallor and the slowly advancing paralysis that was causing the old man's features to relax. He would have noticed the gaping mouth, the glazed and unseeing eyes, the forehead drenched with sweat. But his gaze had been elsewhere and, having failed to notice, his shock was on that account now more extreme.

Lawrence shared it to the full, seeing Gillings grow completely limp and helpless, watching him become first a sagging, intolerable weight in Crawford's clasp and then a still form stretched out upon the floor.

Wordlessly, his lips twitching a little, Crawford knelt and took the stricken man's pulse, gripping his right wrist so vigorously that it seemed improbable that the beats would register at all. It was a mistake and Crawford quickly rectified it by relaxing his fingers a bit, and forcing himself to remain calm.

Apparently there was a pulse, for Crawford removed a tiny physician's flashlight from his inner pocket, and played it over Gillings' pupils, raising first one eyelid and then the other.

He said in a stern whisper to himself, "Must be careful now. Slow—go slow. No conclusions. Test first for congestion; cyanosis. No blood on lips... May not be too serious. We'll see, we'll see."

"Good God!" Jordan exclaimed, crossing to Lawrence's side and giving Crawford a searching look. "Stop mumbling to yourself, can't you?"

The searching look became tinged with a fierce impatience. "Why did you say—about its being serious?"

Crawford looked up quickly, his eyes innocent of anger or resentment. "Can't be sure about anything—until we get him to the hospital. Phone for an ambulance. Hurry, man. Don't just stand there."

His lips tight, Jordan returned to his desk, started to dial.

CHAPTER FOUR

THE SCORPION waited patiently for the elevator at the end of the corridor to ascend to the tenth floor. He looked neither to the right, nor to the left. There was a withdrawn, profoundly thoughtful expression on his face, and even when the elevator door swung open and he stepped into the narrow cage and was carried rapidly to the street his aspect of intense preoccupation did not change.

He walked swiftly along the street that ran parallel to the building's massive graystone facade, crossed at the first intersection, and continued on for several blocks without moderating his stride.

He had crossed the street a second time, and was passing the lighted windows of a large department store when he was startled to see the girl. She had moved very quickly out into the street from the store's main entrance, which was crowded to capacity with men and women shoppers, and was now almost running, the heels of her shoes clattering sharply as she darted past him.

There was a look of stark terror in her eyes. All of the color had drained from her face, and she was clutching a large, black-velvet handbag so fiercely to her breast that her hands seemed like claws, despite their slender, tapering beauty. As he had suspected she'd be from the photographs he had seen, she was a very pretty girl—beautiful, in fact—a little above medium height and with the carriage and perfect physical proportions of a professional model. Her lips were full and curving and almost sensuously over-ripe, suggesting faintly the enticing Scorpion norm in that respect—although she was quite obviously not a Scorpion woman.

She wore no makeup and her hair descended to her shoulders in a tumbled, red-gold mass. As the Scorpion stared she cast a quick, terrified glance over her shoulder and darted closer to the store window, the clattering of her heels on the hard pavement pointing up her fright as nothing else could have done.

Someone shouted at her from the store entrance, but she did not stop. Then a man came into view, heavyset, hard-eyed, with a commanding air of authority about him. He broke into a run even before she did, waving one arm in a peremptory gesture, the muscles of his neck bulging under his too-tight collar, his face turning brick-red in the steady neon glow.

"You won't get away, you—" he shouted. "I saw you lift that bracelet! It'll go easier with you if we talk it over! You hear? I'll catch you anyway—"

The Scorpion moved then. Not to intercept the girl, but to put himself at her side. She was running frantically now and he had to run, too, to keep up with her, despite the length of his stride. She gave a little gasp of horror when she saw him so close to her. She veered sharply and would have dashed out across the street if he had not quickly placed a restraining hand on her arm.

His voice was assured, calm, friendly, despite the urgency of his words. "I'll help you get away," he said. "Just stay close to me and keep running. There's nothing to fear."

For an instant the terror in her eyes seemed to increase rather than diminish, to glow with a taper-flame brightness that gave her almost the look of a marionette dangling from a wire—a puppet woman without volition moving jerkily across a night-black stage, her face illumed unnaturally by light from above.

For an instant she stopped moving, stood motionless in the neon glow. Then a shudder passed over her. The fear did not leave her face, but some of the taper-glow departed. She let the Scorpion guide her, making no attempt to jerk her arm free. Together they darted out from the curb, dodging a passing truck, and pausing for an instant in the middle of the street.

It was the Scorpion who insisted that they pause—he wanted her to regain her breath, to calm down a little more.

The heavyset man was just leaving the curb in pursuit when they broke into a run again.

The opposite side of the street was in striking contrast to the store side, lined with small, three-story office buildings and lighted bars that appeared to be doing a thriving business. A drunken man lurched along the pavement a yard or two in front of them, and from one of the taverns came a loud blare of progressive jazz.

In some strange, difficult-to-explain way the familiar, raucous music seemed to lessen the girl's terror. She turned her head quickly to look again at the Scorpion and the calm assurance in his eyes seemed also to have an effect upon her—a stabilizing effect this time.

He was still holding her arm firmly, but now she seemed grateful for his nearness. As if to make certain that he would not desert her she pressed closer to him.

That simple, instinctive gesture of trust—so natural to a woman in need of masculine protection—seemed to please the Scorpion. For the barest instant a look that could not have been separated by more than a hair's breadth from human warmth appeared in his eyes.

Then the swift approach of the heavyset man brought a sudden change to his expression.

"There's an alleyway just ahead," he whispered. "Two doors beyond that bar. I saw it when we crossed the street."

For the first time she spoke to him. Her voice was in harmony with her face and figure, warm, beguiling, with no fear in it at all now.

As they sped past the tavern the lurching drunk almost collided with the Scorpion but swung about just in time. For a moment his anger flared. "Why don't you look where you're going!" he muttered belligerently. "Shush who d'you think you are?"

The Scorpion paused for the barest instant, looking the man calmly up and down. "You know very well who I am," he said.

The drunk's eyes widened and for an instant his features seemed to come apart. "Good Lord," he mumbled. "It's one of them. A Scorpion! Mister, I didn't mean—Mother of Mercy, what am I sayin'. You're not a 'mister.' You never could be a 'mister.' There's a big difference between every one of us an' everyone of you. We ain't big clocks chimin' out the time until it's too late for any help to come. *You're* big clocks...bang, bang, bang—standing in the hallway...tellin' us our time's about up."

"You should be grateful that time moves very slowly," the Scorpion said. "And it may not be so late as you think. Bear that in mind, my friend."

Abruptly they were moving forward again, the heavyset man almost at their heels now, the blare of music from the bar so loud it drowned out all other sound.

They reached the alleyway and moved swiftly into its deep, enveloping darkness. The Scorpion released his grip on the girl's arm and spoke with quiet confidence, his wide shoulders held very straight.

"You'll be in no danger. Stand well behind me. There is no way I can overcome him with my mind. The time is too short. A mental blow would take minutes to prepare."

Her only reply was a swift intake of breath. He stood as though listening, perhaps to the soft rustle of her dress as she moved further into the darkness, perhaps to the heavyset man's swiftly oncoming footsteps. His face showed no visible emotion beyond a slight tightening of the muscles of his jaw and an increased levelness of gaze that made his large green-yellow eyes seem like the stationary, brightly-burning visual organs of some great alien beast.

The heavyset man was so close now his breathing sounded like two sheets of sandpaper being rubbed together. He was cursing under his breath, and the words he was using seemed to displease the Scorpion, for a flicker of distaste passed evanescently over the alien's face.

He waited patiently, however, until the man had entered the alleyway and was almost at his side.

There was just enough light for the store detective to see the outlines of the Scorpion's face—the eyes certainly—and the formidable bulk of the broad, straight shoulders. He just stood there, breathing harshly, until the Scorpion raised his hand and took a slow step backwards.

Something flashed in the Scorpion's hand. There was a momentary flare, bright, half-blinding, lighting up the alley throughout its entire length. For an instant the detective's features stood out in stark relief, the eyes wide with horror and shock, the jaw sagging as if the ligaments supporting it had been abruptly severed. Then the light went out.

In the returning darkness no darker shadow marked the spot where the startled man had been standing. All that could be seen was a deep shadow at the Scorpion's feet where the detective lay sprawled, his body gone completely limp.

The Scorpion did not move until the girl swayed and clutched at his sleeve. He started then, and looked at her and smiled, and although she could not see his smile his thoughts seemed to wing toward her like slender birds of the night, white-plumaged and swift of passage.

"Is he—badly hurt?" she whispered, her shaken voice barely audible despite the stillness, and the sudden lessening of tension which the Scorpion's utter calmness seemed to turn into an actual bond of strength uniting them, a bond almost physical in its reassuring warmth.

"No—he will recover," the Scorpion said. "I am very glad that we have met."

The girl's hand tightened on the Scorpion's arm. She said, "If it hadn't been for you—" She stopped, then went on with a sudden, wild outpouring of emotion, "I couldn't help taking that bracelet. I couldn't help it, couldn't, *couldn't*. It's an impulse that comes over me. I've been to psychiatrists. They use important-sounding words that mean very little—anxiety neurosis...compulsion...childhood trauma. Something terrible happened to me when I was a child. That's what they'd like me to believe.

"But remembering back—even remembering the things I'd much rather forget—doesn't help me at all. Perhaps I wouldn't go into a store at all if I didn't want it to happen, if deep down in my mind there wasn't something at work that keeps trying to destroy me."

The Scorpion was gripping her arm now, very tightly, shaking her a little. "You'll be all right now," he whispered. "You're safe now. There's nothing to fear. Believe me, the living can be safe too. Men and Scorpions and every living creature throughout the universe of stars. We're still searching for the complete answer...someday we'll know. We have a part of the answer, and I think...the human race has a part. If we fitted the two parts together...who knows? Jagged edges, parts that don't fit exactly, can be smoothed off or replaced...if you've a craftsman's skill."

The Scorpion studied the girl with admiration in his deep eyes.

"Do you know," she said softly, an accent almost of light-heartedness in her voice, "you have reassured me, far more than anyone ever has."

"You have a certain proud independence, a capacity for deep and creative emotion which I like. You were fleeing from something ugly you could not hope to understand. But in every movement of your mind and body I saw—exposed completely in a way that you would not understand—a capacity for light and life and joy."

"Every movement of my *mind*. Surely—"

"Wait, let me finish. Do you know what joy is, in your conscious mind? Can you analyze it, explain it. I doubt if you can. It is something the human race fears, and puts foolishly aside like some frayed and tattered cloak that only a fool would wear. The so-called lower animals know joy. Birds know it, as they mate and burst into rapturous song. They are hot-blooded, intense, eager—tiny bundles of living flame.

"Only Man turns his face from joy. He talks of other things…peace, contentment, hard work, duty. He does not even like to think about joy. But joy alone unites man with the Eternal. In a deep and truly spiritual sense joy is the only human value that enriches human life at every point, and makes intelligent life everywhere in the universe meaningful and—yes, and these are words that I am unashamed to use— noble and creatively justified."

For a long moment there was silence between them. Then the girl said, "You know, you haven't told me your name."

"D'Qy," the Scorpion said.

"Dee-Kee? Dee—"

"No—in English it would be pronounced 'Duke.' That, at least, would be a close approximation. Whenever a man or woman asks me, I say: 'Duke.' But you asked me and I said: 'D'Qy.' Why, I wonder?"

"Perhaps I know why," the girl said.

"Perhaps you do. If you truly do, I am glad. A birth-name has a very special meaning that one likes to keep intact."

The girl said, "I am Ruth Fraser."

"Yes..." the Scorpion said. "Ruth—it would be Ruth. 'She stood in tears amidst the alien grain...' Life has a strange way of bestowing upon each of us a profoundly meaningful name."

The girl's fingers tightened around his hand. "You said just now...you said...you could read my mind."

"No, I said I was aware of the movements of your thoughts. There is a difference, at times rather subtle, and difficult to explain. If you are at all withdrawn from me, or if your thoughts are very important to you and you want to keep them secret, I could not pry if I wanted to. It would go too deeply against the grain."

"Then you are not reading my mind now?"

"No, I am not even making the attempt. If some great emergency should arise, Scorpions could get inside human minds. And once or twice we have. In fact we could, if threatened with destruction, read the minds of every man, woman and child on Earth. But certain conditions must be present—a life-or-death urgency—a deep-seated, almost compulsive need. And we must have time. It cannot be done on the spur of the moment."

The Scorpion looked away for a moment.

"Between Scorpions the *rapport* is stronger. Even then we must have time, but I have now had sufficient time. The car is at the end of the block. It will be here in a moment."

Ruth Fraser started and released his hand, drawing a little away from him. "The car? I don't understand—"

"If you are frightened...you have only to tell me and I will get into the car alone. You have absolute freedom of choice. The thought of forcing you to do anything against your will would be intolerable to me."

"You mean—you want me to go with you?"

"Yes," the Scorpion said. "If you are not afraid, if you completely trust me. Not otherwise."

"But why? Where are you taking me? What...will happen to me?"

"Nothing you need fear. I am going to try...to set you free. You are imprisoned in a cruel web. The psychiatrists you went to couldn't help you because they are themselves imprisoned. Their science is worthy of respect, precisely as the smooth, skillfully polished flints of the caveman are worthy of respect. But polished flints cannot unlock the energies of the atom, and are best looked at in museums. Modern psychology here on Earth cannot unlock the massive doors the human mind has built up around itself through a thousand generations of groping in the dark."

There was a sudden flicker of light opposite the alleyway, a dull, steady droning. The long Scorpion car had glided so smoothly in toward the curb that it seemed almost to materialize out of the darkness, its brightly-polished hood mirroring the tavern lights as it came to a full stop directly in front of them and abruptly ceased to vibrate.

The door of the driver's seat opened and a Scorpion got out. He was taller than Duke—and leaner, more methodically light-footed, and agile in aspect. His face was heavily lined but he moved with the spryness of a young hawk trained to descend with a lightning-bolt efficiency upon its prey.

But as he crossed the pavement in three short, swift strides Ruth Fraser did not draw back. Miraculously, all of the fear had left her. The Scorpion's eyes were level and kind—there was no threat in them, no menace.

Duke moved quickly forward to greet him, clasping his hand in a completely traditional human manner, and then slapping him lightly on the shoulder in an equally comradely way.

"We're going to have a guest for a few days," he said. "This young lady needs help—needs it desperately. She can help us immeasurably…in ways that are more important to us now than ever before. We still do not know…*why human beings behave as they do.* It's as simple as that. And she's as tortured inwardly as any human woman I have ever talked to—more tortured."

The Scorpion from the car looked at Ruth steadily for a moment. Then he nodded, and said enigmatically, "Perhaps we can help her. Perhaps she can help us."

CHAPTER FIVE

THE WALLS WERE as smooth as the walls of a stone prison, the windows as high and narrow. But it was not a prison and could never be.

Duke paced the floor of the high-arching meditation cell, drawing strength from its severity, its bareness. There was no furniture at all in the cell, not even a chair. The walls mirrored Duke's image as he paced and the image seemed almost to become momentarily that of a human monk, dedicated to austerity.

Nothing carnal can into this high sanctuary intrude...

The balance, he thought, the occasional swing of the pendulum from joy to complete austerity. Yes, it has its therapeutic value. But we are not foolish enough to regard it as an end in itself. What it does is strip the mind bare, harden and toughen the will. But there are other, better ways...

He remembered a human fable, amusing now because it seemed so apt, so completely in accord with his present mood. A man hits himself on the head with a hammer, over and over again. Then he stops. "Why did you stop," someone asks. "Why? Because it feels so good when I stop."

Could austerity increase joy? Could it lead to a heightening of joy when you stopped?

There were men and women of his race who thought so, and the educational theory had been allowed to creep into Scorpion culture to this very slight extent. There were and probably always would be meditation cells.

She would be under hypnosis now. Truth serums first, and then hypnosis. And they'd probe deep.

Why, why, why? The simple question—why? A woman so beautiful, so young—why wasn't she filled completely with the joy of life? Why did she inwardly torment herself? Why did all human beings torture themselves?

From birth to death, never a moment free from inward torment.

The psychology of the criminal act. Not the thought, but the act. Consider that for a moment. No man would commit a crime if he was completely happy. Yet all men commit crimes in their thoughts. Scorpions do not, but men do.

Frustration? A shallow Earth term, lacking breadth and vision. It went deeper than that—

Ruth Fraser moaned and opened her eyes wide. The first object she saw was the metal headrest of the couch, curving out so far on both sides of her head that its gleaming upper portion was visible to her.

The bright shimmer of light on the surface of the curving, wedge-shaped prongs dazzled her eyes for a moment. Then her vision grew accustomed to the glare and she could make out the broad, straight outlines of the Scorpion's heavy shoulders, and even the outlines of his face, which had seemed at first a part of the dazzle. The Scorpion was not Duke.

Gradually as she stared up the Scorpion's face assumed firmer contours. The high cheekbones stood out prominently, like a miniature mountain range on a broad expanse of very wrinkled flesh. The deep-set eyes grew darker and more piercing and the mouth took on an aspect of sternness.

Then, abruptly, the Scorpion was smiling at her—nodding his head and smiling. "We have made considerable progress," he said, reaching out to pat her on the arm. "I believe we are getting somewhere."

Ruth gasped and started to rise, but the Scorpion took her firmly by the shoulders and eased her head back upon the bed rest again.

"You mustn't try to get up now," he cautioned. "You'll feel dizzy if you do. Suppose you just rest and let *me* talk to *you*."

She could see the far wall of the room now and the strange and alien-looking instruments of science that were ranged along it. She was almost sure that they were medical instruments, but she could not be entirely sure. They were certainly quite different from ordinary human hospital equipment or the equipment she'd seen in doctors' offices as a child, and later, as a desperately troubled and ill—quite ill—adult.

The Scorpion was speaking to her now. He seemed neither young nor old, but in some strange way almost ageless. His eyes were trained steadily upon her but there was nothing frightening in his gaze. On the contrary, there was in the warmth and sympathy of that steady regard something that seemed even more than reassuring.

"You told us a great deal that we needed to know about you," he said. "As a child you thought and felt very intensely. We have our own techniques for measuring intelligence, but the human ones are accurate enough as far as they go. By human standards you have an I.Q. of one hundred and forty, which is just comfortably below the human genius level. But feeling—aesthetic and emotional sensitivity, that's the important thing. Imagination, intellectual daring.

"Let me put in this way. On Earth we've discovered that genius-level I.Q.'s—one-fifty to one-seventy—are a drug on the market. I'm using a terrestrial colloquialism, but I'm sure you'd understand it quite as well as we do, even if I put it in slightly different terms.

"It's what a capacity for intense feeling can do to those I.Q.'s that's important. Any human being—man or woman—with an I.Q. of one-seventy who's also emotionally dead, a cold fish, a clod—just isn't great as we would define human greatness. He does not increase the amount of joy in the universe by one iota. But a man or woman with a very modest I.Q.—say one-twenty, or even one-ten—can be one of the shining ones of Earth."

The Scorpion's expression grew more intense. "If he or she is abnormally sensitive and emotional the I.Q. can be set aflame—can glow with ten thousand new and daring colors. We have studied human greatness on Earth very painstakingly. One of the greatest of your painters—a Frenchman—was actually only one stage removed from an idiot. But the joy in his canvasses made him immortal."

The Scorpion's eyes were glowing now. "You—as a child—were abnormally sensitive, imaginative and emotional. And because Man fears joy—you were condemned from the day of your birth to be an outcast."

"Then that—"

The Scorpion nodded. "Yes, that is the reason. You were different and from an early age you found all hands raised against you. Even a strong man would have been hard put to defend himself, to retain his sanity. You were a woman."

"I see..." the girl murmured. "At least...I think I do. But why did I always feel so *guilty*. And why did I want to do—hateful things?"

"Because you are human. When a man or woman cannot give creative expression to the joy he was born with his thoughts turn to destruction. It's as simple as that. If you build something joyous and beautiful and everyone ignores it and in addition, accuses you of being a fool, or a criminal, you *will* become a criminal."

"And you...can cure me. If I stay here with you I will be cured?"

"We have laid the foundations, my child. There is much that we do not know, vast, uncharted areas that we must still explore. But...yes, I think we can help you."

Ruth Fraser turned her head then, quite suddenly, and saw that another Scorpion had entered the big, quiet room with its many alien instruments, and flame-strange brightness.

For an instant she did not recognize him, so bright was the flare of light at his back and so unfamiliar and unusual his garb. He was dressed entirely in black, in a garment that resembled a monk's cassock, close fitting and reaching almost to his feet. It was belted in tightly at the waist and flared at the shoulders, which were additionally draped with a more abbreviated, circular garment which enveloped the back part of his head and spread out over the upper part of his back very much in the manner of an ample, loose-fitting cowl.

For a moment his gaze rested upon her, while he held himself very straight, his eyes considerate, solicitous, his arms folded on his chest. He seemed to be awaiting her recognition, his whole attitude that of a concerned onlooker who admits to being deeply involved and does not wish to intrude at the risk of administering the slightest additional shock.

Suddenly the anxiety left his face and he nodded. "Yes, I can see that you are quite all right. The hypnotic techniques we decided on are not dangerous in themselves, but there are occasionally temporary side effects that take hours to vanish."

"D'Qy, there are no side effects that this young lady could not cope with," the other Scorpion said, his grave, kindly countenance breaking into a smile. "She has done splendidly. And we've learned a great deal about her childhood that we needed to know."

Duke nodded and drew closer to the couch. The girl returned his stare with a fragile eagerness.

"Duke," she said, and the words sounded perfectly natural on her lips, as if she were addressing some old human friend who, almost overnight and through some bright miraculous sharing of a secret known only to the two of them, had become most precious.

He bent closer to her, his hand going out to grip her shoulder with firm reassurance. He felt suddenly very happy. There was the fragrance of a summer garden on his home planet, the bursting of purple seeds, the unfolding of petals, the smell of newly turned earth. Far off the sea thundered, its high bright surges loud in his ears.

"I am quite all right now, Duke," she said. "I have begun—to understand why I am as I am. Deep down in my mind the guilt feeling, the torment, is still there, but it does not seem nearly so bad now. I can endure it because I know...there is hope for me."

"More than hope," Duke said, his eyes very steady.

Ruth Fraser rose from the couch. She was surprised by her own calmness, the ease with which she descended to the floor and stood facing Duke and the other Scorpion.

"I'm quite all right," she said. "There is no dizziness."

Duke looked at his companion, and his voice was low when he asked, "Would it be safe—to show her Base Unit Seven? I should like her to see a few projections, the general scope and groundwork of our plans. I think it will reassure her. There's an Earth expression I've always rather liked. 'At home.' I should like her to feel completely at home with us."

The other Scorpion nodded. "She may find it difficult to remember she is still on Earth. You may have to keep reminding her that nothing has changed—that outside this building the cherry trees of Washington are still in bloom and that men and women are still walking in and out of the Government buildings carrying briefcases.

"She knows nothing of large-scale interstellar projection. She has never seen Scorpions, moving vehicles, vessels at sea, spaceships in a thousand-foot vault—a projection composed entirely of light-transmitted energy and yet as real in aspect, as three-dimensional, as the objects themselves. She has never moved in and out of a light projection and become a part of it, a woman of flesh and blood moving in another world, another universe.

"She may become frightened, stunned. She has never walked through the rooms of a completely transparent dwelling, descended a flight of stairs as firm in structure as the floor of this room, and stared out through a pane of glass-simulating energy at a landscape on another planet, projected across thousands of light years.

"She will need to be reminded that the building itself is no more than a projection, matter-energy in flux, and that the breeze that is stirring the trees beyond the window has never blown over the green hills and valleys of Earth and that the trees themselves have not grown like an oak from an acorn but have reproduced themselves by a process unknown on Earth. The trees, rivers, valleys, cities will chill her with their strangeness, terrify her perhaps.

"Her mind has not been properly prepared, so it will be a risk. Are you prepared to take it—on your own responsibility? I have no power to command you. You are your own master. You must decide for yourself. As your friend I can only advise and urge caution. Young and inexperienced eyes have looked before now on wonders too deep and vast for the star's cavern of young minds to grasp."

Duke said, "I think that she will have the courage to look calmly across space at our world and accept what she sees there without becoming in any way disturbed. All life is strange. That life should have come into existence at all on a spinning mote of mindless matter in space is strange beyond belief. That it should exist on ten thousand planets throughout the universe of stars is even stranger. The simple fact of birth prepares every human being for a life of exploration, of uncertainty, of fearful risks undertaken with a stout heart.

"If some of us recoil before the challenge—others do not."

He was looking at Ruth Fraser now, an apprehensive expression on his face. "Will you trust me and take the risk? Scorpions are completely human, even though we have been called aliens, visitors from beyond the stars, even—invaders. Even though we have been called *creatures*...we are men in the fullest sense. We take pride in the fact that we can think, feel, act in such a completely human way...and that even our blood types are similar to yours. Parallel evolution is no myth. Creative intelligence has everywhere in the universe clothed itself in much the same garments.

"The lower forms of life may differ slightly, on every inhabited planet throughout the universe of stars, but the evolutionary process has everywhere culminated in a big-brained biped with almost godlike gifts of intelligence—a fragile, almost hairless biped with the lightning at his fingertips, and an ability to transcend his immediate environment in ways that are strange."

Ruth's hand crept into his. "I am not afraid," she said. "If you have an unknown world to show me, let us go and look at it together."

CHAPTER SIX

JIM LAWRENCE sat alone with the Bureau Chief in the big silent office, a gray light at his back—the light of dusk, undoubtedly, but somehow more unnerving than any such light had a right to be, more *coldly* gray and unnatural looking.

The ambulance had come and gone, but the departure and hospitalization of Gillings had not diminished the tension in the least. If anything, the horror and uncertainty had grown.

"Gillings must have started sagging the instant the Scorpion stepped into the office," Lawrence said. "I'm quite sure he didn't say a word after that. I wasn't watching his face at the time, but we hardly need a diagram. That Scorpion *did* something to his mind."

"Isn't it just barely possible that the blow you struck him—" Lawrence shook his head. "A delayed concussion? No. If I seriously thought that I'd go out and shoot myself. But I refuse to believe it. I struck him on the jaw for his own protection, because I had no alternative. But it wasn't a brain-injuring blow. A man has to jar his skull pretty hard to produce even a light concussion, like—well, falling against a curbstone."

Harvey Jordan nodded. "I never really doubted it. I just wanted your opinion."

"Here it is, then—in full. The Scorpions, as far as we know, have never before attempted to influence the human mind telepathically. We had no reason to believe they possessed ESP powers at all—certainly not to a dangerous degree. But what happened to Gillings seems to prove otherwise. I believe that two separate attacks were made on Gillings' mind, in an effort to silence him.

"The first attack, in the swamp, produced amnesia—the peculiar mental state of 'glory' Crawford described. But under hypnosis a part of that mental block was stripped away. Gillings remembered, and talked. But I'm almost certain Gillings didn't remember and couldn't inform us of *everything* he saw when he approached the wrecked Scorpion spaceship. And that's why a second attack was made upon him—a half hour ago in this office."

The Chief was staring very intently at Lawrence now. "Yes," he said. "I'll buy that."

"The second attack was made because the Scorpions realized that the amnesic block had broken down. Another exposure to hypnosis, and Gillings revelations might have become complete enough to seriously endanger their plans."

"I'll buy that, too," Jordan said. "We've done some speculating about those plans, and added it to what we know. The sum total was frightening enough to justify our sending for you. But before we talk about that, I'd like to ask you one more question."

The Chief's lips curved slightly upward, but there was no real mirth in the smile. "You had the look of a wide-eyed schoolboy while Crawford was talking, but you didn't deceive me for one moment. I happen to know you could talk circles around him when it comes to psychology. You know a hell of a lot about medical diagnosis, too."

"Just from reading," Lawrence said. "Just as a layman, I assure you. The average pre-med student could talk circles around me if I—ah, well skip it. Just one thing, though. The correct term is *physical* diagnosis."

"See what I mean? Well, anyway, there's something that puzzles me. I thought extra-sensory perception *wasn't* inverse to the square of the distance. I mean if the Scorpions actually can get inside our minds and produce paralyzing changes why couldn't they do it just as well from a distance? I'm thinking specifically of the *second* attack on Gillings. Why did that Scorpion have to come here in person?"

"Well, for one thing, it would take a very powerful ESP impulse to influence or damage the cranial nerves at the base of the brain and produce an actual paralysis. The cerebral cortex itself is a quite different matter. ESP, as we've observed its manifestations in men and women, seems to function through some kind of super-dimension, independently of space and sometimes of time, directly on the higher centers. But even there, where the nuclei of the motor nerves and the nerves of special sense originate, not strongly enough to produce any pronounced physical trauma.

"Further down, below the cerebral hemispheres proper, in the cerebello-pontine angle, the nerves are infinitely more robust and resistant. To produce an actual paralysis of the nerves at that point the ESP potential would have to be tremendous. And Gillings apparently suffered the kind of 'stroke' that goes with severe cerebral nerve damage—or, at the very least—temporary paralysis. Crawford wasn't sure. But I was almost sure, just from looking at him."

Jim Lawrence's expression became more somber. "That brings up an even more important point. We don't know precisely what kind of ESP ability the Scorpions may possess, or just how it functions. It may be quite different from the rudimentary human ESP faculty."

"So the Scorpion had to be near Gillings to throw him into a coma," Jordan said. "Is that what you mean?"

"Yes—in a general way. Quite possibly Gillings had to come close to the wrecked Scorpion spaceship before even the amnesic block could be imposed. We've no *absolute* assurance that telepathy on any level is completely independent of space and time. In the early Duke University ESP experiments considerably better results were obtained when the sender and the receiver of the messages were in fairly close proximity. In the case of more highly developed telepathic faculties close proximity could be even more important. The more advanced and specialized a faculty is—the more limited it often becomes in general scope."

"Sounds logical," the Chief said. He stood up. But he did not move away from the desk, simply drew a little back from it as he pulled open one of the spacious drawers. From the drawer he took a small, camera-like instrument and placed it on the desk.

The instrument was less than eight-inches square, compact and very beautiful. It was a man's delight in aspect—an artist's delight, a skilled mechanic's delight. The male human animal likes to tinker, likes marvelously constructed mechanical parts, gadgets that are a miracle of beauty and precision. This was such an instrument, blue-enameled, expensive looking, flawlessly assembled.

Lawrence could not tear his eyes from it. So absorbed, indeed, did he become that he was startled when the Chief clicked it on, and light and color flooded the desk.

Light and color, movement and sound. On the desktop the main street of a small country town stretched out, throbbing with all the vibrant hues and textures of life itself. Men, women and children passed up and down the street, crossed at an intersection, paused to window-shop. The curbs were lined with cars. From one of the stores a man emerged and drove off. Another man, in a gray business suit and a briefcase under his arm, entered a two-story office building beneath a hanging sign that read: *John Jepson, Attorney-at-Law.*

A child clutched a bobbing red balloon, and turned to stare at a passing poultry truck. The heads of geese craned and twisted between the slats of a wooden crate, and there was a distinctly audible *honk.* A teenager in dungarees passed down the street whistling. Two girls stopped to stare after him, giggling. A wolf call came from the door of a poolroom. A gas station attendant paused in his high-octane labors to swab a perspiring brow.

Color, movement, sound and familiarity. Lawrence caught his breath and his throat tightened with the wonder of recognition. There had been changes—many changes. But it was still *his* town. It was still the little Vermont town in the valley that had been his parents' home and his own during all the years of his boyhood. Even some of the faces were familiar to him, despite the changes.

Even the Scorpions could not change the minds of men and women quite so appallingly. And yet the changes were not all for the worst. In some of the faces, where once he had seen only a dull lack of promise, there now shone forth dignity and strength and a fine glow of accomplishment.

Then Jim Lawrence saw the Scorpion. He was walking alone near the far end of the street, a strikingly handsome individual with dark hair and eyes, and an unusually slender build for a Scorpion just a little past his first youth—a Scorpion, in short, of about his own age.

As Lawrence stared down, still feeling the slight constriction at his throat, one of the passers-by turned and nodded at the stranger in their midst. Lawrence could hear the words of the greeting quite clearly. "Good afternoon, Duke."

"Good afternoon," the Scorpion replied and continued on.

"Gillings mentioned that one," Jordan whispered, his fingers nudging Lawrence's sleeve. "Apparently he's won a great deal of local liking and respect. At the very least—respect."

Lawrence turned, his lips white. "I don't understand. What *is* this? A three-dimensional projection of some sort, but good lord—I've never seen anything so lifelike!"

"I'll explain in a minute," Jordan said. "Watch…"

Almost infinitesimally tiny seemed the many hurrying

figures, and yet each stood out distinctly, as did the miniature storefronts and parked cars. The illusion of immediate, flesh-and-blood reality was so complete that Lawrence scarcely dared raise his voice for fear of being overheard.

The Scorpion woman appeared quite suddenly on the street, emerging from one of the stores only a few steps behind the solitary figure of Duke. She moved quickly forward to join him, nodding and smiling at him in a quite casual way, as if she wished it to be known that she was merely confirming the bonds of a valued friendship with graciousness and restraint.

She was barely more than a girl and her beauty was—breathtaking. Her eyes were large, lustrous and very dark, and shaded by long, curving lashes. Her high cheekbones gave to her face a slightly exotic cast, as did her over-full lips. But when she smiled that faint alienness of facial contours was forgotten and even when she didn't, it hardly seemed to matter. Far more would have been required to mar her beauty even slightly in Lawrence's eyes.

Another farm truck rumbled past, blotting the two Scorpions from view for an instant. When it had passed Lawrence caught a brief, final glimpse of them disappearing down a side street.

Almost immediately after that, people on the street began to waver and grow dim. A haziness enveloped the storefronts and spread out over the entire scene. It was accompanied by a stillness and a receding murmur of barely distinguishable voices and after a moment even that faint undercurrent of sound was gone.

The entire street vanished, to be replaced by a dull flickering that caused Jim Lawrence to look up quickly, dazed incomprehension in his stare.

"You'll see the ship in a moment," Jordan said. "Don't look so startled, Jim. We could never assemble an instrument like this, but we've come pretty close to it. It's simply a three-dimensional image projector—or rather, a camera and projector combined—that creates an illusion of reality with great depth and color and vibrancy to it. The sound synchronization may seem a little on the miraculous side, but apparently it's not beyond the scope of Scorpion technology.

"The voices are in some complex way magnified, each voice distinct in itself, impinging on the ear with an almost unbelievable sharpness and clarity. The images, too, are a little sharper than they would be in life, but that only seems to heighten the illusion. Their tininess is somehow made negligible. The scene grips and possesses you so completely that you become a part of it. You seem to be seeing and listening to life-size men and women. The human brain, remember—and this undoubtedly applies to the Scorpion brain as well—creates its own size orientations to fit the occasion."

The Chief nodded thoughtfully. "I'll give you an example of this. Wear very strong magnifying glasses for a time, and then take them off abruptly. You'll still see images that appear to be magnified, larger-than-life images. The brain has automatically made certain readjustments, ignoring the actual image flashed to it by the retina of the human eye."

Lawrence scarcely seemed to be listening. So extreme was his state of blindly groping bewilderment, amazement and shock that only one of Jordan's statements had registered with anything like a normal impact. That statement now occupied his mind to the exclusion of all else.

"You said...*we* could never assemble an instrument like that. *Then this—is not a human instrument?*"

Jordan shook his head. "No. It's a Scorpion instrument. I thought I made that clear. Right after the Gillings' tragedy alerted us we threw all of the resources of three Government departments into the job of at least *trying* to get our hands on something concrete. Before the hypnosis experiment with Gillings was even attempted—while Crawford was experimenting with the truth serums. One of the Bureau's own men—Ralph Summers—lifted this camera-projector from a Scorpion who just happened to be dozing after a heavy meal in a roadside tavern. It was an almost incredible fluke of circumstance."

The Chief smiled grimly. "The Scorpions are human enough in a good many respects. I don't need to tell you that. I was watching you just now, when you saw that Scorpion girl." The smile vanished. "Scorpions, as you know, even get drunk, lower their guards, have at times an almost irresistible desire to be liked. Even by us—that's the strange thing. To be liked with an almost pathetic, childlike intensity at times—unbelievable in a race so advanced. Possibly it's because a desire to be liked is the most deep-seated craving of biological intelligence everywhere in the universe.

"Psychologists tell us that even hate—cruel aggression—stems from a frustration of that basic need, that overwhelming emotional craving not to feel rejected, or spurned. People hate because they are unable to make themselves liked. The roots of that need may lie even deeper than the simple phrase 'desire to be liked' suggests. It may go back to the first primitive beginnings of unicellular life—to the organism's need for security and friendship. But we needn't go into that."

The Chief's eyes hardened and at the angle of his jaw the small, mobile muscles bunched into knots. "But we must be careful. We'll be making a mistake if we lower *our* guards."

"They're being lowered—all over America," Lawrence said, a stunned shakiness in his voice. "Just why did they make a recording of that street scene? Have you any idea?"

"Well—we've given it a great deal of serious thought.

Quite possibly they wished to make a special recording of their last days on Earth, as a kind of historical summation, something to refer back to a century or so from now. But it could just as easily have been made as a kind of—well, emergency test run. Something of great and urgent importance to them is going on near the wrecked spaceship.

"There was one ghastly accident, apparently, as you'll see in a moment. Perhaps they wanted to attach a street scene to it, taken at random in the immediate vicinity, to enable them to test out some special feature of it. Or it may be no more than what a laboratory technician would call a 'precautionary control'—a manifestation of their extraordinary thoroughness in conducting any kind of experiment."

JIM LAWRENCE suddenly found himself watching the flickering again, startled by the streaks of jet blackness that were creeping into it. As he continued to stare the streaks resolved themselves into trees, their enormous boles spaced at sentry-like intervals around a forest clearing. In the midst of the clearing the wrecked Scorpion spaceship leapt into sudden prominence, its long, cylindrical hull enveloped in slanting shafts of moonlight.

Lawrence had known the setting as a boy, and it took him only an instant to recognize it. Hillsdale Wood, the sloping stretch of dense trees and grassland a few miles to the east of the town. Only the ship was new, an intruder on the sylvan solitude. The descent of the ship had charred the great oaks close to it, and had channeled a deep crevice in the earth that was steep-walled around its entire circumference.

There was no stir of movement about the ship, no sound at all. Only absolute silence and stillness, as if some unseen presence had commanded the forces of nature to be silent. The very absence of sound was unnerving, so startlingly did it contrast with the hurry and bustle of the familiar street scene of a moment before.

The ship did not fade as the street scene had done, to be replaced by a new and completely different setting. The image simply shifted, as if the recording instrument had become an aerial camera. The trees changed, thinned and grew thick again, and the ship itself was quickly lost to sight in a vast sea of greenery.

It was not until then that Lawrence became aware that Jordan was standing very close to him, his breathing distinctly audible in the silence. "I told you there was—an accident," the Chief said, his voice low, oddly strained. "The first time I saw it I was pretty badly shaken up. You'll see it, too, in a moment. Just thought I'd better warn you..."

For a fleeting instant Jim Lawrence saw only the trees and another sloping expanse of charred earth. Then the camera-eye of the recording instrument seemed to shift abruptly, and a portion of the slope that had been invisible before came sharply into view.

Lawrence's breath caught in his throat. The slope looked desolate and bleak in the gray light, but the shape that towered there was not a natural part of the desolation. The shape was that of a wildly rearing horse, its mane distended, its teeth exposed and gleaming in the moonlight. Its front hoofs were thrashing at the empty air, frozen to immobility and yet unmistakably thrashing, precisely as a figure carved in stone by a master sculptor may convey an illusion of constant motion despite its absolute rigidity as an object of art.

There is a marble stillness that lasts forever and yet is as short-lived as a dropped heartbeat, for the human imagination alone can endow cold stone with sudden, pulsing, vibrant life. But no imaginative effort was needed here, for the horse was—or had been—alive.

It was impossible to believe otherwise. Its straining flanks were ridged with a rippling interplay of muscles which no sculptor, however great, could have hewn from a block of stone with absolute, camera-like accuracy—even had he so desired. And what sculptor who was not also a fool would have attempted any such thing? The function of art was to interpret reality—not to copy it line for line, displaced hair by displaced hair.

All that flashed across Jim Lawrence's mind as he stared down at the rearing horse. Partly it was a protective rationalization, and effort to escape from the immediate horror of the scene itself, to blot from his consciousness, if only for an instant, the spectacle of a frenziedly trapped animal frozen to immobility in a wholly unnatural way.

The rationalization was logical enough and almost certainly true. But there was more to it than that. He was experiencing, in addition, the quite ordinary shock reaction the human mind undergoes when it is unexpectedly confronted by an enigma, a challenge, a mystery almost beyond sane belief.

Was the horse still alive, or had it died before the Scorpion recording instrument had swept down over the hillside? It was difficult to tell. Possibly it was merely paralyzed with shock, held rigid by terror and might at any moment recover from its fright and go plunging on through the woods.

Could a dead animal maintain such a posture—upright, unmoving, its forelimbs rigidly extended? Could a dead animal still seem to be thrashing with its hooves at the empty air? Could rigor mortis be as sudden as that, as profound and all-embracing, all apart from the impossibility of rigor overtaking a man or animal in such a position?

It seemed impossible and yet—not only was the horse unnaturally rigid and unmoving. From its head to its tail it was enveloped in a glow—a bright, steady radiance that clung to it like a shroud.

The scene was starting to flicker and grow dim, precisely as the village street had done, when Jordan spoke again.

"We've run that recording off at least a hundred times," he said. "We've studied it from every angle, speculated about it and reached a conclusion which seems inescapable. Something killed that horse with an almost lightning-like swiftness. Just before it reared up it may have had its neck bowed, pawing the earth. Fright alone may have caused it to rear up. But something more than fright killed it."

"Are you sure it's dead?" Lawrence heard himself asking. "For a moment I thought—"

The Bureau Chief gestured impatiently. "Wait, let me

finish. There's only one explanation makes any kind of scientific sense. *Radiation.* Not the kind of radioactivity which would register on a Geiger counter, perhaps, but radiation notwithstanding. You saw the glow!"

It wasn't a question, exactly, but the Chief paused as if expecting a reply. When none was forthcoming he went on quickly, "A strange, new, deadly kind of radiation capable of paralyzing or killing instantly, capable of turning a horse into a rigidly contorted, brightly glowing animal mummy. Statue of stone might be a better way of phrasing it. Figuring it out will be a problem for the experts...if it happens again and we find the animal."

Jordan was suddenly intense. "Do you realize what this could mean? You know what happened to that South Pacific island seven years ago. If what we suspect is true, the Scorpions may be experimenting with an even more dangerous kind of radiation—something they *can't* control—or can't be sure of controlling.

"It's a possibility we can't ignore... It seems extremely likely that the horse was killed accidentally—by some kind of energy seepage from the wrecked spaceship, during the course of their experiments with a new fuel. Adding it to what we already know and suspect—the information we've gathered, the Gillings tragedy—we'd be justified, I think, in reaching such a conclusion."

The desktop scene had vanished completely now. The light had gone, and the small Scorpion projection instrument had again become an object of simple beauty with mirroring surfaces—blue-enameled, intricately compact.

The Chief's expression grew more decisive. "Look at it this way. That horse and the wrecked Scorpion spaceship were in close proximity—less than eight hundred feet apart. The recording instrument moved from the wreck directly to the horse, as if the vicinity factor had an important bearing on what took place. Now—we have reason to believe that some very special kind of research activity has been going on board the wrecked ship. Doesn't it seem likely that an accident may have occurred, and that the recording was made—at least in part—to guard against similar accidents in the future?

"I'm getting back here to my test-run theory. The Scorpions probably make careful recordings of everything that takes place when they conduct an important research experiment."

"Yes," Lawrence conceded, his pallor still pronounced. "It seems logical enough."

"The horse may have been killed by a radiation seepage acting gradually upon it until it finally reared up and became rigid in that ghastly, unnatural way. But I believe that the end came more quickly...that it was killed by a single lethal shaft darting out from the wreck."

The Chief nodded, letting out a long breath, as though his mind had settled the matter to his complete satisfaction in at least that one respect.

"Whatever happened, it does have an accidental look about it. Call it a hunch, if you wish, an inspired guess. But what I'm going to tell you now lends a great deal of support to it."

Jordan returned to his desk and sat down. He gestured Lawrence toward the chair directly opposite him. "I'll give it to you straight, Jim," he said. "And I'll make it brief."

Lawrence nodded and sat down opposite the Chief, realizing that Jordan would not have spoken with such crisp deliberation if he had not been completely sure of himself.

Jordan began with a question. "Tell me, Jim. Just what do you know about the Scorpion spaceship? What *did* you know—before you listened to Gillings' outburst, and what I've just been telling you?"

Jim thought for a moment.

"Not too much. I knew, of course, that they had made a kind of tourist attraction out of what's left of it. Not the Scorpions, but the townsfolk, from the mayor on down. Visitors were at least permitted a fairly close look."

"Not any more," Jordan interrupted. "The Scorpions exerted pressure in a mild, friendly, local way. Just mild Scorpion pressure always seems to be enough. I don't know, exactly, what strings were pulled—because we've been deliberately holding off investigating that particular aspect of it. Asking questions in Quarry Hill will be *your* job."

Lawrence looked startled. "My job! I'm afraid I don't—"

"Forget about that for a moment," the Chief interposed sharply. "Pretend I didn't say it. I take it, from what you've just told me, that you knew nothing about the wrecked spaceship beyond the fact that it was a tourist attraction until about two weeks ago."

Lawrence nodded. That's right. My knowledge ends there."

"You didn't know, then, that the Scorpions put in a request for Sodium FE-438 with the Atomic Research Control Board right here in Washington. You know, the fusion element Scorpions use to fuel their stardrive?"

"No, I didn't."

"At that time—it was about five weeks ago—they pretended to be in complete sympathy with the tourist attraction idea. They claimed they wanted to make their grounded spaceship look real for the yokels."

A slight smile flickered across Lawrence's face, but the concern did not leave his eyes. "I think I understand," he said. "The Scorpions get a few grams of FE-438, put it, shielded, into the fuel chamber, and let the sightseers peep at it, through a ten-inch-thick quartz window. But then the A.R.C.B. turns them down and they use ordinary baking powder instead."

Lawrence's features tightened, and all of the levity went out of his voice. "I just don't get it, though—not any part of it. They have plenty of Sodium FE-438 fuel."

The Chief shook his head. "We don't think so. We think their fuel supplies may be running short all over Earth. They may not have enough to power the stardrive of a single ship for the long journey home. We think they may be experimenting with a *new* fuel—an atomic development that will enable them to use the small amount of FE-438 they can get from us in combination with some new fissionable product, a thousand times as powerful."

In every line of the Bureau Chief's body, in the way he spoke, was a desperate earnestness impossible to misinterpret.

Lawrence said, "You mean they're using that wreck as an experimental laboratory? In a larger sense—using *Earth* as a laboratory?"

"That's exactly what I mean," Jordan said. "Can you think of anything more potentially dangerous? Their own South Pacific Island demonstration would be a child's toy by comparison. And they'd just naturally be reckless with a planet that doesn't belong to them. As for blowing *themselves* up—well, we don't know enough about their psychology to be sure they can't take even self-destruction in their stride. They may welcome it, glory in it.

"For all we know, they may have a suicide complex. Like—well, remember those Japanese fliers in World War II? The individual doesn't matter—only the race, the nation. An alien behavior pattern could be even more irrational."

"So they wanted some of our FE-438," Lawrence said. "But they didn't get it, did they? Frankly, it doesn't make sense to me. Why should they use such a flimsy, transparent excuse in an attempt to get it? To make the wrecked spaceship a more convincing tourist attraction? Why should they want to do that particularly, especially since they knew they'd have to keep all tourists away from the ship in another two weeks anyway? What high-placed Government official here in Washington would believe such a story?"

"Someone believed them," Jordan said. "A sentimental, civic-minded fool on the Atomic Research Control Board. I'm not at liberty to disclose his name, but they used just the right approach with him. They convinced him that making that wrecked ship a more realistic attraction would increase goodwill all around, and make the Scorpions seem more like public benefactors. We admire men of great wealth when they endow museums and restore historical sites, don't we?"

"Then they *did* get some FE-438?"

The Bureau Chief nodded. "They got it, all right. And it wasn't just a matter of a few grams, either. They probably still have a supply of the stuff themselves, in the other ships, but they apparently need more from us, as fast as they can secure it. Next time they'll think up some new excuse—or take it by force."

Jordan arose and walked to the window. For a moment he stood with his back to Lawrence, staring out over the city of Washington that somehow seemed imperishably beautiful in the deep purple dusk. He could not see the dome of the Capitol, only lighted buildings stretching away into the tremendous and onrushing night.

As he stood there he seemed, for a moment, one with the great multitude of men and women who had walked the streets of the city in generations that were now forever joined to yesterday's ten thousand years—no, to the billion years that had elapsed since the Earth had cooled and the still warm seas had given birth to life.

He returned abruptly to his desk, sat down and faced Lawrence. "You were born in that town," he said. "You were born in Quarry Hill, Vermont. You spent your boyhood there. And some of the men and women you knew as a boy would greet you if you returned almost as if you had never been away. To most of them you would still seem a boy—older, taller, wiser but little different from your younger self.

"The years do not change us so very much, Lawrence. People we have known from birth become a part of our deep, subconscious selves, and remain always young in our eyes, always unchanged. And we in turn still seem young to them. I am glad that we do."

The Chief smiled. "Strange…that is not really what I intended to say to you at all. Wait, though…perhaps it is, in a way. There are thousands of trained investigators here in Washington. We could send them swarming over Quarry Hill with microfilm cameras and concealed notebooks, and a most persuasive disguise. They could become schoolteachers on vacation, tired business executives, high-pressure salesmen, clerks, with a genius for fly-casting, golf-fiends, antiquarians.

"But they would not have the *feel* of the town, Jim—not understand its texture, the throbbing, tumultuous pulse of its inner life. They would be greeted by everyone as strangers, and in a small country town all strangers are suspect, even the most friendly and easygoing and likeable, even the hail-fellow-well-met. Do you understand what I'm driving at, Jim?"

Lawrence stood up. "I think I do," he said, remembering back. Remembering the gray Victorian house that his grandfather had built for three generations of Lawrences, and the well in the back yard and the winding country road just beyond. Remembering his first day at school, the tears, the sadness, the storm that came up, darkening the panes of the schoolroom, remembering Molly Rubeck.

Remembering as well the frog in the lunch basket, the

picnic table gaily spread, the grammar school diploma he'd clutched so proudly, the hard-knuckled fist fight with the town bully, the sodas in the drugstore, the high school swing orchestra, and the flat-brimmed sailor straw with its blue and orange band.

And now everywhere across the land it was still happening and the world of the very young remained unchanged— despite the coming of the Scorpions and the fear and the dread in the eyes of the not-quite-so-young and the middle-aged and the very old.

Jim Lawrence knew then what the Chief expected of him and what his answer would be.

CHAPTER EIGHT

DUKE LOOKED thoughtfully at the woman who was walking with him across a room that had ceased to frighten her—away from the couch where she had reposed and been helped by the silent Scorpion healer.

"If you have an unknown world to show me, let us go and look at it together."

He seemed to be turning the words over in his mind and suddenly he said, "For months now we have been conducting tests-screenings—to determine what men and women have the vision, the endurance, the strength of purpose to help us in the great task we have undertaken. Perhaps 'search' would be a better word. We have searched far, and now at last we have found the right kind of human material. Human nature is very much the same everywhere on Earth. But we thought it best that the men and women we select should each have a different heritage. You, too, are one of the strong ones."

Ruth Fraser turned and looked at him, her eyes wide, incredulous. "Strong? After all that I told you about myself—"

"Yes. Your great imagination, your capacity to feel deeply and intensely—are in themselves manifestations of strength, the only kind of strength that is important. I have decided to trust you completely. You will be the first—to see what the Scorpion civilization is like.

"We have selected, from many nations, a small group of men and women—unusual in every respect. One is from a little town in Vermont called Quarry Hill. Another is from England, another from France, another from the Soviet Union. There is a South African pygmy, and a Chinese explorer in the group. The selected men and women are unusual in almost every respect—intelligent and imaginative beyond the average, with a deep capacity to *feel*.

"You, too, have been selected. We have been studying you, observing you closely, for some time. I came to Washington for two reasons. One concerns our immediate security and does not involve you. The other was—*to contact you*.

"The contact came a little sooner than I expected. I was approaching the store because I knew you were there. If I had not encountered you as I did I would have sought you out in your lodgings a few hours later. But I did not know— before I met you—that I would be so instantly drawn to you. The rapport between us appears to be even deeper than I had thought it would be."

Ruth was astonished to learn that she had been singled out by the Scorpions—but was no longer startled by anything Duke might choose to reveal.

Together they walked across the room and out through a door that opened silently at their approach. They moved down a long, blank-walled corridor, and descended a flight of narrow stairs lighted from above by circular lamps that glowed with a pale blue radiance.

The stairs were very steep, lined by handrails that mirrored the lamps in a quiet astonishing way. Like stars the lamps seemed, glimmering in the constantly deepening shadows— stars that seemed almost to be following them as the long, crystal-bright rails guided them past convolutions as intricate as the interior structure of some vast seashell, opalescently gleaming in a cavern measureless to man.

Down and down they went, Lilliputian figures descending through a Gargantuan whelk's house of lime and star-mirroring crystal, their steps echoing hollowly as they passed from light into shadow and then back into light again.

There were brief intervals when dazzling light seemed completely to envelop them, and yet the darkness remained in the ascendant—so much so, in fact, that the shadows seemed almost to have a strange, greedy life of their own, darting toward them from all angles even when the light half-blinded them and feeding, leech-like, upon the light, absorbing it until only a dull gray flickering remained.

Down and down until, finally, the stairs leveled off and they were walking straight out across the floor of a completely featureless vault more terrifying in its immensity than the whelk's house of descending convolutions had been.

The floor of the vault was translucent and it shimmered with a rainbow iridescence, each spectrum hue separate and distinct. There were banners of red, green, blue and a dozen colors that were either neutral or achromatic—not just white, black and gray but seemingly a blend of each with something new and strange added—a brightness such as neutral colors were not supposed to possess.

It was almost as if the light that never was on sea or land, the incredible light of the poets—of Wordsworth and Coleridge and Blake—had crept into the vault and suffused it, turning even the blacks and grays prismatic, and giving to even the light-diffusing colors the aspect of a lens that was also a wheel of fire.

So immense was the vault that Ruth could not see across it. And when she raised her eyes the roof was swallowed up in a flickering emptiness, consisting of shadows perhaps, or consisting of no more than the nebulously weaving obscurity which great height and distance imposes on human sight.

Then before her eyes an object took shape. It was white and circular and of no great height and she could see at once that it was a building with windows and a doorway and that on its sloping roof there had been erected what appeared to be an aerial transmitting instrument of some sort—an intricate network of wires and gleaming metal rods supported by a sturdier and starkly simple framework of forked metal poles.

The Scorpion spoke then for the first time. "We will walk together into the house," Duke said. "It is really a house of a thousand windows, because the view beyond the one window will change constantly. The house will travel, it will move from place to place. It was not built on Earth and it is not on Earth now. What you see is a light-projection, transmitted from my home planet across space."

He nodded, his fingers tightening on her hand. "It is a house of light and yet it is three-dimensional, substantial, as firm as the flesh of my hand. The walls are constructed of energy-matter in flux, and as you move through it, energy that has not quite become matter will make solid the floor beneath your feet."

The interior of the house did not even seem alien. It was too completely featureless in every way, the lower-floor rooms opening directly on a terrace that was enveloped in a swirling iridescent mist.

"Duke—" the girl said, and stopped.

"Yes." Duke looked at her. "You spoke of a window. What does that terrace open on?"

Duke smiled and said, "On nothing at all. The house is in stasis now. It is not moving yet... The room and window are upstairs. Come."

The stairs were narrow, firm, compact—not at all like the whelk-shell convolutions that had made Ruth's temples throb and fear to increase within her until she had almost succumbed to an impulse to cry out and turn back. There was security here—of a sort. The very smallness of every-thing, the blank walls, the solid cornices, the total absence of furnishings of any kind made it seem like a doll house enlarged just sufficiently to accommodate adults—a trim dwelling fresh from the carpenter, uncompleted as yet, with a fireplace that lacked a flue and with wood shavings on the floor.

The upstairs room was astonishingly small. The ceiling was low and the walls less than ten feet apart. It was a completely square little room and the one small window was also square. It appeared to be paned with glass that had an almost fragile look.

Beyond the pane there was only a swirling grayness, no different from the mist which had enveloped the terrace on the floor below.

The Scorpion still held firmly to Ruth's arm. Without a word he drew her toward the window and said, simply, "Look."

Slowly the mist began to dissolve. Rents appeared in it, weaving patches of light brighter than the iridescence.

Gradually as Ruth stared the bright patches widened, dispelling the mist on both sides of the pane, rolling it back in luminous bands.

Beyond the pane stretched a terraced garden, purple-garlanded, beautiful beyond belief. Tall, violet-red plants, their stamens tipped with radiance, marched in double file across a snow-white stretch of masonry, and descended a moss-covered slope to a fountain with seven jets, each golden and shaped like a flamingo in flight.

In the middle of the terrace, between the tall flowers, two Scorpions were walking slowly back and forth. One was a male, a little younger than Duke and the other was a slender, dark-haired woman, her eyes languorous and golden in the waning sunlight.

"They are very happy," Duke whispered. "Completely relaxed. They are in love, you see, in a quite simple way. There is no need for them to torment themselves, as men and women in love must always do on Earth. They are not torn by indecision, by jealousy, by fierce doubts. They do not have to ask themselves, 'Is this really love? Will it last? And where will my beloved be a year from now? In the arms of another man?'

"They are completely sure of each other, completely sure of themselves. They are sure because the fire within them burns so brightly and steadily. They are consumed by it, although you might not think so to look at them. They seem to be in love in a completely passionless way, but that is not really true at all. The opposite is true. They do not need to embrace with an outward display of passion because the joy that unites them is a living flame. It is all consuming. It cannot be fanned to a greater brightness and any attempt to do so would be fraught with danger."

"Danger?" Ruth whispered. "I don't understand—"

"There is always danger in exhausting an emotion, in trying to pass beyond it," Duke said. "Joy itself—free and unconfined as it is—is hedged about with explosive tensions. When the cup is full to tamper with it is always dangerous."

"And we on Earth—you think we have tampered too recklessly?"

"I do not know. We would not have remained on Earth if we had been completely sure of the answer. There is perhaps some one thing you can teach us—a way, a means, a salvation. For at one vital point we are grievously stricken, and facing possible annihilation."

"You—the Scorpions?"

"All of us, yes. Watch now. The house is moving. You will see that all joy on my home planet is not the quiet, self-contained joy of two lovers walking together in a garden. There may be more symbolical truth than you think in the primitive terrestrial folk-myth of the serpent and the garden. They partook of the forbidden fruit and a new world of joy unconfined burst upon their startled vision. Lilith, remember, was also in that garden—the sweet soft woman who entwined herself about Adam and then gave birth to demons."

The scene beyond the window was changing rapidly now. The terrace had vanished and a shining road appeared, wider and more resplendent than the roads of Earth and so flawlessly integrated into the landscape that it seemed a miracle of engineering genius—a construction feat, indeed, that defied analysis.

It stretched away into purple distances, across miles of virgin forest and gleaming silver lakes, its every elevation a harmonious curving. Like a dancing note on a musical score it seemed as the house followed it, leaping in sonic joy over all obstacles, rising to a crescendo of onrushing hills and descending with an arrow's swiftness into deep purple valleys.

Presently a city came sweeping toward them, its spires golden in the purple desk. Into the city the house passed and down a street lined with white stone dwellings with oval windows and wide, high arching doors.

Male and female Scorpions moved in and out of the houses, crossed the street singly and in pairs, stopped to exchange greetings, and to watch children at play. They looked up at the sky as if fearful of a storm. Some of them paused to pat small, furry, large-eared animals whose exuberance, shown by their wagging tails, seemed to match the man-loving friendliness of the dog.

The Scorpions moved with great animation their faces radiant, as if just being alive was the rarest of privileges and a source of never-ending joy. Every movement they made seemed to give them pleasure, every word they spoke to increase that strange fellowship of intense inward happiness—a fellowship as strong, certainly, as the bonds of human friendship but more abounding in carefree give-and-take, more completely the servant of joy.

The window seemed to mist for an instant, to become

almost opaque. Then the street scene vanished and the dazzling whiteness of a great stadium swept into view, causing Ruth Fraser to draw back and stare at her Scorpion companion with a swift intake of breath.

In the midst of spiraling tiers of Scorpion spectators five separate athletic contests were taking place. Could that vast amphitheater have been transferred to Earth it would have made the Roman Coliseum seem like a midget ruin unworthy of a second glance, the Yale Bowl a toy structure. But it was not so much the size of the building, but the games, the contests themselves, which widened the girl's eyes as she stared.

Never had human prowess on Earth displayed such strength and endurance, such resilience and bodily grace. Never had the surrender to the physical been so complete, so absolute, never had skill pitted against skill, agility against agility, experience against experience scored triumphs so spectacular, a joy so all-embracing, a satisfaction so miraculous.

Naked youths and maidens raced shoulder to shoulder across a white stone track, hurled discs with more than Grecian grace, high-vaulted with the soaring ease of birds in flight. Lithe-limbed youths in the lightest of armor fenced and sparred with rapiers that glittered like diamond-studded scimitars in the down-streaming light. Others batted brilliantly colored balls into basket-shaped nets, leapt over hurdles, dived from a high platform into a rectangular pool and swam with vigorous, overhand strokes toward an illuminated victory-marker, which glowed blue and ruby-red.

It was a spectacle that dazzled the eyes, bemused the senses, a paean to joy and victory acted out with ten thousand bodily movements, perfectly coordinated, lightning swift. Applause thundered between the tiers, penetrating the thin glass pane, echoing throughout the house.

Louder and louder it grew until, abruptly, all sound ceased. The pane clouded again and the bright, stupendous vista was gone.

Ruth Fraser was afraid now. She dreaded what she might see next, as if obscurely aware that her human brain could absorb just so much bigness, vastness, splendor and must recoil in bewildered torment if the newness and the strangeness became too great—became, in fact, an act of outrage.

Duke seemed to sense this fear in her. He seemed to understand how it was that she could tremble and turn pale when she had remained a spectator solely, and when he spoke again his words were tinged with solicitude.

"You must not let the Scorpion way of life frighten you," he said. "We live with both our bodies and our minds, in a harmonious worship of joy. All experience is to us a living flame that takes complete possession of us in early childhood—almost, in fact, from the moment of our birth. We are taught in the nursery to rejoice in the great gift of life itself, to hold everything else secondary.

"Because we have been so taught, we are a deeply reverent people. We have a deep reverence for all life and yet a great tragedy has come upon us. We do not know why. We are still seeking an explanation. You have seen what joy can mean when it has been accepted by an entire race as the greatest of life's gifts. Now you will see the other, darker side of the coin.

"You will see our stricken villages. You will see listlessness, hopelessness—a melancholy and a black despair so inexplicable that we can hardly reconcile it with what we know of reality. It has descended upon us like some great, rapacious hawk of the night. It is an illness of the spirit, a plague of the mind that has spread from village to village and left a third of our people desolate."

The window was becoming bright again. There was a stir of movement, a shifting of perspective, a change in the gradations of light and shadow just beyond the pane.

A village street came slowly into view. It was lined with low, conical buildings constructed entirely of stone, but looking more like igloos in their architectural symmetry, their monotonous uniformity of design. The buildings ran parallel for perhaps three hundred feet, and then branched and dwindled as the street itself forked.

Before several of the dwellings gaunt skeletons sat— Scorpion men and women so emaciated they seemed little more than mummies sitting upright in the sun. Their eyes bulged glassily and from their ash-gray faces, deeply lined with wrinkles, most of the expression had departed, leaving only a kind of grooved-in apathy, a frozen despair.

Even when one—a male—arose and tottered a few paces, as if the weariness and life hatred which rested upon him had become a burden too intolerable to be endured, there was no change in his expression, no animation in his dully roving stare.

Almost immediately he sank down again, and another mummy-like figure struggled to its knees, stretching forth a skeleton-thin arm for a bowl of food which rested on the discolored paving stones at its side.

"They have lost all desire to go on living," Duke said. "They have food in abundance but they seldom eat and they could not be worse off if a famine had descended on the village. They sleep only when absolute exhaustion overcomes them. A fever consumes them but it is not the fever that living imparts. For them life has lost its meaning, its savor. They are like dispirited children in a dark room, forever cut off from the light. They are the living dead and we can do nothing for them. All joy has vanished from their lives and we do not even know why."

For a moment there was a strange, brooding stillness up and down the street. Then the sunlight shifted a little and one of the half-somnolent mummies came to life again. Energetically to life this time, leaping to his feet with a grimace so tormented, so despairing that the girl at the window was filled with an instant foreboding, a conviction that something terrible was about to happen which she would be powerless to prevent.

Ruth Fraser could not tear her gaze from that tortured Scorpion figure, even when he whipped a knife from his belt and held it upraised for a moment, steady and gleaming and with the blade pointed directly at his chest.

He brought the knife down with a single, violent contraction of his arm, almost as if some invisible force had taken possession of him, steeling his muscles and his will and committing him irretrievably to an act of violence that would put a swift end to his wretchedness.

For an instant he swayed with the knife buried deep in his chest, his lips trembling, shaking, as if he were summoning his last reserves of strength for a final outcry, a malediction directed against life itself, a curse that would linger on after his own passing and be taken up by more and more of his people, until the last Scorpion city had crumbled into dust. Then the glaze that sheathed his eyes deepened and a dull red stain overspread his chest. His knees sagged and he fell and lay prone, with one thin arm outstretched as if at the very last he hadn't really wanted to die.

Ruth Fraser covered her eyes with her hands and screamed.

CHAPTER NINE

"WALK THE HILLS, Jim. Tramp the valleys. Renew old acquaintances, seek out old friends. Be completely yourself. Do not hurry like a man rushing to catch a train, or a man in love late for a date. This is too important, too urgent. If the enemy is coming at you, laying down a steady barrage, you must be very calm and relaxed. Otherwise you will not move nearly fast enough."

The Bureau Chief's words echoed in Lawrence's mind as he descended from the train at Quarry Hill, walked with him across the crowded station, and hovered persistently at the edge of his consciousness as he tipped a redcap to retrieve his luggage and was driven in a ramshackle, 1987-model coupe to the River View Inn.

He registered for a single room with running water, large, airy and sunny, and went to bed the first night without announcing his arrival to anyone.

At cock's crow the next morning he was up and about, and events moved rapidly after that.

The friends of his boyhood were the first to welcome him, but there were many others who wanted in on the act, for a native son does not return every day in the week.

He soon got to know the town's leading citizens and some who were not so leading and a few who were furtive and difficult to know and a few who fraternized with Scorpions and spoke to them perhaps more frequently than was deemed wise by the majority.

He even struck up a nodding acquaintanceship with three Scorpions—it would have seemed strange if he had not done so—and was a little surprised to find himself being greeted by them with a pleasant nod when he went walking along Main Street, his eyes squinting against the bright New England sunlight.

Day by day his contacts and his interior wisdom grew. Old folkways came rushing back to surround him with a warm glow.

In no time at all he was a bred-in-the-bone citizen of Quarry Hill again, privileged to go into a hardware store and purchase a fishing lure from a frog-eyed little proprietor who could have himself passed muster as a lure for a very big pike, privileged to exchange church gossip with Miss Brooks and Miss Lucy White. And not forgetting, of course, that he was not a church-going person himself, privileged to greet Judge Hawkins in a busy tavern taproom with a "How'ya, Dick," and even to drop in at the Sheriff's office and ask Deputy Bill Ragout precisely what he thought of big city dicks.

"Don't think much of them," had been Ragout's answer. "Don't think too much of you snooping newsmen in Washington either. In this town it's the Scorpions, though, who do most of the snooping. Don't see why we'd need a detective, big city or small town, to come here and tell us how to run things—if we ever did have a murder, or anything really serious."

It was that conversation that led to Lawrence's first important lead—and his last lead of any kind on Earth. Yet it began casually enough, with Ragout's big, bony frame silhouetted against a sun-dappled windowpane, his brown hickory features drawn together in a scowl that seemed, somehow, distinctly amiable.

So pronounced, indeed, was that amiability that it was impossible for Lawrence to take Ragout's comment seriously. From the first there had been a humorous twinkle in the man's eyes, a satiric twist to his lips. Quite obviously he did resent out-of-town snoopers. But not to a really serious extent and he was clearly willing to waive the way he felt to put Jim Lawrence at his ease.

"We haven't had a murder in this neck of the woods for ten years," he said. "Forget I even brought the matter up."

"I was the one who brought it up," Lawrence said, quickly. "Do you mind if we carry it a step or two further—in a more realistic direction. I've been puzzled by one or two things that seem to be happening here with the full knowledge of everyone—things that are disturbing enough to cause a great deal of uneasiness.

"But no one seems to want to talk about them. At least, they won't come right out and talk about them, won't volunteer information. You can understand my position. I'm as much of a native son as anyone could be, but I also happen to work for the Government."

"None of us hold it against you," Ragout said. "Even a village sheriff works for the Government. We'd all be in a bad way if we didn't."

"That I can understand. But I'm supposed to be here on vacation. And I *am* here on vacation. I came back to relax and have fun. I came back because I was born here. Isn't that easy enough to understand? Why should the whole town be suspicious of me?"

"They're not, Jim. No one is suspicious. But when you ask too many questions you rub people the wrong way."

"I see. Well, that's what I want to avoid. Being human, I have a certain natural curiosity. I can't completely repress the way I feel. I wouldn't have any fun at all here if I tried to. It's one thing to vote with the town, to go along—quite another to realize everyone you meet knows something you don't."

"I wouldn't put it that way exactly, Jim."

"How else can I put it? Look, I'll give you an illustration. Say you're a popular guy, you're invited to a party. Someone comes up and gives you a glass of sherry. Someone else hands you a sandwich. You have the sandwich in one hand

and the wineglass in the other. Then a big blue-bottle fly lands on the back of your neck and starts to annoy you. What can you do? You can't so much as raise your hand to flick the fly off."

Ragout sighed. "Okay, Jim. You win. What is it you'd like to know?"

"The Scorpions don't actively interfere with law enforcement here in the village, do they, Bill? Actually pull wires and that sort of thing?"

"Not directly, no." Ragout's expression became abruptly thoughtful. "Not directly—but they do exert influence. The Sheriff knows more about that than I do. I'm just a deputy, remember. My job doesn't take me too far afield. I've never had a private session with the mayor, let alone the governor."

"But you do know that the Scorpions exert influence. Quarry Hill's chief pride and glory was that wrecked Scorpion spaceship. It brought tourists here in droves, gave a tremendous shot in the arm to local business. But now the Scorpions have taken it back again. They've—well, roped it off. To all intents and purposes they've attached a sign to it labeled: *No trespassing. This ship is Scorpion property.*"

Ragout's lips tightened. "That's true enough," he said. "But after all, the ship *is* their property. They've let it be known that they've taken it back only temporarily."

"But why isn't there more indignation, a bigger protest? Why is everyone so afraid to even discuss it?"

"Why don't you ask Washington that, Jim? It's something that concerns the entire nation. That ship was a tourist attraction, in a way, for every man, woman and child in America. Even when they couldn't come here and look at it they could think about it."

"I understand all that. But right now I'm chiefly puzzled by what's going on right in Quarry Hill. Why the evasiveness, the refusal to— Oh, well, you know what I mean. I've met several Scorpions since my return and talked with them. They're more open and above-board about what's going on here than the men and women I knew when I was a kid. They didn't tell me anything I didn't know—just that they were planning to ship some of the wreck's damaged instruments to their base in England, and needed elbow room while they worked on the job of dismantlement. Hence the 'no trespassing' move.

"That's understandable enough. It made sense to me. What didn't make sense was the fear in the eyes of every native son I talked to about it. I can recognize fear when I see it, especially in the eyes of a Vermont-born man. We're not the kind of people who frighten easily."

Ragout looked at Lawrence steadily for a moment before replying. Finally he said, "Would it surprise you if I told you that ship isn't quite as 'roped off' as you seem to believe? I've never had any desire to visit it myself. I could give you several names, though, of people who feel very differently about it, who have been willing to take the chance. The Scorpions invited them and they went. They've returned safely to their homes, and there's no longer any fear in them."

Lawrence was too startled to say anything.

Ragout regarded him speculatively for an instant, then went on, "I guess the man you should see and talk to is Mark Whitsun. He's fairly new to the town—came here about six years ago. He manufactures antique reproductions—has a little factory just the other side of the railroad tracks. He's closer to the Scorpions than six or seven others I could mention. And those others have been close enough. He doesn't fear them at all, and if he doesn't think you've an ax to grind I'm pretty sure he'll take you into his confidence."

Jim Lawrence stayed in the Sheriff's office for only a

minute or two longer. He knew he'd have plenty of time to think over what Ragout had told him during the ten or fifteen minutes it would take him to drive across town to where Whitsun's business sign swung to and fro in the breeze, and he didn't want the deputy sheriff to regret his startling candor and become evasive again.

He could visualize Whitsun's sign before he saw it, perhaps from memory, for he had walked more than once up the narrow street where the furniture factory was bringing the past very color fully back to life. MARK WHITSUN—ANTIQUE REPRODUCTIONS.

A big, rusty sign, swinging in the breeze, the lettering slightly chipped. Yes, he could remember it, all right. But when he actually arrived before the low stucco factory structure he was surprised to discover that someone had scrawled in colored chalk beneath the old English lettering: *Scorpions Welcome.*

It was quite obviously a schoolboy prank—too malicious to be in the least amusing. Obviously, too, it was of very recent date, or Whitsun would have discovered and removed it.

Lawrence descended from his car, and walked swiftly up the graveled pathway to the factory door. The Mark Whitsun who came briskly into the small reception room a few minutes after Lawrence had given his name to the receptionist looked very much like—an antique manufacturer.

He was below medium height, and his chestnut-colored hair, which was thinning on top, half-covered his forehead in a circular, antiquated bang. He wore a stained brown smock, and had the long-fingered, sensitive-looking hands of a skilled craftsman. His eyes were blue and very piercing, his mouth in character, being large, and relaxed, but purposeful, as if at a moment's notice it could become tight-lipped and in entire conformity with the owner's sharpness of perception as he concentrated on some difficult task.

He said, "Good afternoon, sir. I don't believe we've met, but I do know who you are. Jim Lawrence, isn't it?"

For an instant a disturbing thought flashed across Lawrence's mind. Had the little antique manufacturer been expecting him? It seemed unlikely and Whitsun's next words dispelled all of his doubts on that score.

"You can't return to the town where you were born without creating something of a stir, particularly if you've been away for a good many years. I've passed you on the street perhaps a dozen times but I doubt if you so much as noticed me. I noticed you, however, because your name was on everyone's lips. You must have been a very popular youngster and spent a very happy childhood in this town."

Despite the seriousness of his mood Lawrence's features relaxed in a responsive smile. The little man's friendliness seemed completely genuine and would have been a difficult thing to counterfeit.

"Well, I did spend a happy childhood here," Lawrence said. "As for being popular—I'm not so sure. I was a sensitive, rather withdrawn youngster, although perhaps you wouldn't think so to look at me now. I can still recall a fight I had with the town bully. I more than held my own, but I didn't enjoy it. I was a reader and a brooder—a dyed-in-the-wool introvert until I became a Washington newsman."

"We all change," Whitsun said, his eyes sparkling as he returned Lawrence's smile. "When I was a youngster antiques were dusty, unpleasant objects stored away in my aunt's attic. I avoided the slightest contact with them. I was something of a hellion, I'm afraid. Enjoyed getting into scraps and—yes, scrapes. Took Dutch leave from school whenever an urge to go fishing came upon me. Probably broke a half-dozen windows with carelessly hurled baseballs."

He nodded and the sparkle in his eyes became a steady,

bright taper glow, as if just thinking back was a joy and a solace to him.

Then, all at once, the sparkle vanished and he looked at Lawrence very earnestly and inquiringly. "Just what did you wish to see me about? If you're interested in my reproductions I'd be delighted to show you through the factory."

Jim Lawrence shook his head. "No, it isn't that. Frankly, I don't know just how to begin. In some ways I feel like a fool."

The sparkle was back in Whitsun's eyes again. "Don't begin then. Just tell me. Plunge right into the middle of things. There's a Latin phrase for it. *In res media*—or something of the sort. I never was much good at Latin."

The little man's amiability was so contagious that Lawrence relaxed a little. "Okay," he said. "Perhaps that *is* the best way. It concerns the Scorpions—their influence in Quarry Hill, their completely unpredictable behavior. Bill Ragout told me you're on very friendly terms with them. To put it bluntly—he told me you know quite a few of them and feel completely relaxed and at ease in their presence."

Whitsun did not seem in the least disconcerted by the statement. "And why should I not feel at ease," he said. "I'm convinced they wish us well. They are more human and downright friendly than most people realize. I've enjoyed talking with them, getting to know them better. They trust me completely because they know I've no particular ax to grind."

Lawrence hesitated for an instant, as if fearful that Whitsun might think that exactly the opposite was true in his own case. The fact that he had a very sharp-bladed ax to grind must, at all costs, be kept carefully concealed.

"I suppose I may as well be completely frank," Lawrence said. "I'm such a curious-minded jackass that I could lose my job by over-reaching myself. I didn't come to Quarry Hill on assignment. I've no license to meddle. But just as a human being, as a native son, I feel cheated, left out of things. The Scorpions have denied access to the wreck to everyone—or almost everyone.

"Bill tells me you've actually visited the ship in the company of Scorpions. Quite obviously you didn't see anything there of a very disturbing nature, or you wouldn't be standing here now defending the Scorpions.

"Just what did you see—and why did you go in the first place? If you don't want to tell me I'll understand. I've no right to ask. I'll say that again. No right at all. No one in Washington is standing behind me. But I would like to know. Does that make any kind of sense to you?"

Whitsun looked at him very steadily for a moment, running his fingers through his thinning hair, disarranging the bang. Finally he said, "It makes a great deal of sense. Intellectual curiosity for its own sake is the rarest of human gifts. I admire a man in whom it flames strongly and brightly."

"Thanks," Lawrence said. "I *am* curious, believe me."

"And experiencing something very close to mental torment because there is a big, disturbing, unanswered question in your mind. Don't imagine for a moment I can't understand that. I experienced the same kind of inner torment myself until the Scorpions decided to be completely aboveboard with me."

"Then—"

Whitsun nodded. "You've asked me a question. I'm going to answer it in a very direct way without hedging or keeping anything from you. There is nothing in that wreck we need fear."

Lawrence made no reply. He merely waited, sensing what

Whitsun had not finished, that he would have to go on. If he failed to do so he would lay himself open to a charge of evasiveness, the very charge he had taken great pains to deny. He would be in the position of a man who has promised much, and in almost the same breath refused to divulge anything at all.

"You look disappointed," Whitsun said, as if aware of Lawrence's thoughts. "I assure you I've no intention of misleading you. You want proof and you shall have it. Right now, this very moment—if you're prepared to put aside certain misconceptions you seem to have regarding the Scorpions. If you can overcome your perhaps understandable dread—or, at the very least, hold it in abeyance—I'll take you to the Scorpion ship. I'll take you there and you can see for yourself."

"Good Lord!" Lawrence heard his own stunned voice as though from a distance, remote, incredulous. "How can *you* take me there? Everyone in Quarry Hill has built up a great wall of mystery about that ship—for two or three weeks now. You mean...we'll just walk up and go inside, as though we were out for an afternoon stroll?"

Whitsun nodded. "Exactly. A stroll—or two glasses of nutbrown ale at the Quarry Hill Inn, unless you prefer whiskey-and-soda. There's a tang in the air, the foliage is at its best, and it's a fine day for a hike. It will be as simple as that. The Scorpions will be most unlikely to undermine a trust they've built up with patience and forbearance and a great deal of give-and-take on both sides.

"They trust me and are justified in doing so. They'll trust anyone I may choose to bring with me. And I—well, I happen to like you, Jim Lawrence. I like the cut of your jib. I like you and I believe in your basic integrity. I know you wouldn't lie to me."

For an instant Lawrence had an impulse to blurt out, *But I am lying to you. Damn it all, can't you see that? It goes against the grain, but I've no alternative. The security of our world is at stake. If you knew you would understand.*

He conquered the impulse before Whitsun made it a dead issue by affirming in a matter-of-fact voice, "I won't be a moment. I don't want to walk through the village in this smock. They have me tagged as pretty much of an eccentric as it is. No sense in adding fuel to the flames."

IN THE BRIGHT, early afternoon sunlight, the scarred and blackened earth immediately surrounding the Scorpion ship did not seem quite so much of an alien desecration as Lawrence had imagined it would become when the distance factor had been removed, and he found himself within thirty or forty feet of it.

He was walking now over the very ground he had traversed a hundred times in imagination and had looked down upon from the high, rocky slope above a half-dozen times in reality. Always by moonlight and with a frightening sense of *aloneness* and encroaching peril urging him to take no chances, to turn about and beat a hasty retreat before it was too late.

Curiously enough, he experienced no such dread now as he approached the ship with Whitsun at his side. Even the towering bulk of the long, cylindrical vessel, with its blue-gray, dully-gleaming hull and shark-finned side vanes, did not cast a pall upon his spirits. The ship's nearness and its structural alienness seemed somehow integrated into his experience. There was no fierce tempest of dread and uncertainty, only awe and the feeling that something tremendous was about to happen.

Not even Whitsun's somewhat hesitant manner caused him any alarm. That his companion should approach the ship with caution seemed entirely natural, for was he not putting an incredible friendship and trust to the severest of all possible tests? An uninvited human guest was bound to arouse concern in an alien mind, no matter how far the barriers had been lowered, the difficulties smoothed over.

He was not surprised, therefore, when Whitsun said, "Walk slowly, keep close to me. They know we are here but we must not seem to hurry. They must not be allowed to think that you have influenced me in any way. We must seem to be approaching the ship together, as old friends, in a perfectly casual, unhurried way."

"Sure, I understand," Lawrence said, and moderated his stride accordingly, looking up with admiration as they approached the cylindrical vessel.

It was his last conscious act on Earth.

CHAPTER TEN

SOMETHING INCREDIBLY bright and shining seemed to rise up directly in Jim Lawrence's path and hover for an instant before his dazzled vision. Then it swept down upon him, enveloping him in a steady, gentle warmth, irradiating him from head to foot. The sensation would have been a comforting withdrawal of all tension from his body, a radiant enfoldment no more harsh than a caressing wind if it had not robbed him at the same instant of all capacity to feel.

For a very long time Jim Lawrence felt nothing at all. And with the departure of all sensation, from mind and body his human awareness flickered and went out. The cells of his brain suffered no damage, but they ceased to transmit thought impulses from nerve ganglion to nerve ganglion, and he did not even dream.

He remembered nothing, *was* nothing.

To emerge from a deep, dreamless sleep to light and sound and color, to experience, even before awakening, an awareness of self, of identity, to recapture, even in the distorted mirror of some almost intolerable nightmare, one's own very special and precious identity can be—is, in reality— an act of creation.

The sleeper awakens and recreates himself.

To Jim Lawrence the process was a long and agonizing one. At first his mind seemed to have been split up into a million pieces, each one limitless in extent and having no definable gradations. Each fragment seemed to flow, to stretch out endlessly. Each fragment was a sea without a shoreline, with no jetsam on the tossing waves, no buoys to make the channels, the deeps, the shark-infested shoals.

Then each fragment became an exploding and expanding universe. Slowly from the arms of spiral nebulae individual suns split off, coalesced into a single bright star cluster, and filled all space with a steady, downstreaming radiance. Even more slowly the radiance became the mind of Jim Lawrence, his consciousness, his restored awareness of self.

He sat up and looked about him. He felt no dizziness, no shock reaction at all. His mind was clear, his perceptions unimpaired.

He saw at once that he was in a small, square compartment, blank-walled and completely featureless, except for a wide circular window that glimmered in the light of a somewhat smaller overhead lamp, also circular. Both the window and the lamp were embedded in the interior structure of the room, the lamp directly overhead and the window at shoulder-level in the metal wall surface directly opposite him.

With a shock he realized that the walls were vibrating.

The throbbing was so low, steady and continuous that for an instant its significance did not dawn on him. He simply arose, experiencing no vertigo, walked to the window and stared out, still under the spell of his first, almost automatic survey of his surroundings. The solidity of the compartment and its imprisoning smallness were clear in his mind. The rest remained hovering on the edge of his consciousness until—

He saw the stars! Through the window they gleamed—pinpoints of shimmering radiance in an ebon vault. In one corner of the sky they swarmed together like golden bees but there were solitary wanderers, too, and one so large that it dwarfed all the others, a stellar giant with a visible corona and prominences that reached hungrily out into space.

Lawrence's shoulders jerked and he took a faltering step backwards, a great, despairing cry welling up in his throat as the ship zoomed close to the great star. Its huge, gaseous body now filled the window. Lawrence turned his back, a look of terror on his face, and at that precise moment a panel in the wall opened—a Scorpion stepped into the room.

For a moment the Scorpion stood motionless, his eyes on the portal and the stricken man. Then he stepped quickly forward and grasped Lawrence by the shoulders.

"There is nothing to fear," he said as the spacecraft flew by and then gradually away from the stellar giant. The two men shielded their eyes from the brightness. "We are in outer space, but we are in no danger. We have taken the first, important step by perfecting a new fuel. Our supply was running short, all over Earth. But now we have enough new fuel to take this one ship back to our home planet. Do you understand? We bear you no ill will. And the ship is safe—completely repaired. This journey's success is assured."

Lawrence turned slowly, his first shock already eased, but willing to let the Scorpion think that his words of reassurance had accomplished their purpose. Let the Scorpion take the credit. Pride, standing on a minor point of human prestige, no longer seemed important somehow. There was too much at stake, the blow that had been dealt him was too terrible and irremediable.

In some obscure way he even felt grateful to the Scorpion, though he should have felt only bitterness and rage.

"You have not been harmed in any way," the Scorpion said, his voice earnest, compelling, deeply sympathetic. "We simply made you lose consciousness with—well, a technique we have. Just one of several minor medical techniques for producing complete anesthesia. We knew that you would not come with us willingly. So we implanted in your mind a suggestion, a hint. Because of that suggestion you called at the Sheriff's office and talked with Ragout.

"Ragout's mind, you see, was also prepared, made receptive. We instructed him to refer you to Whitsun. Our influence over Whitsun was even more pronounced. He did not lie to you. We have taken him completely into our confidence because we found him unusually receptive and a quite remarkable man in a good many respects."

"Remarkable," Lawrence heard himself protesting. "You mean as a *slave?*"

The Scorpion shook his head. "No, he is not a slave. Just a clear-thinking, highly intelligent man whose mind happens to be exceptionally accessible to us. We can influence all human minds if we have to—but it is very difficult in some cases and takes a great deal of time. Whitsun was responsive from the first. Just as Gillings was responsive. But even Gillings we could not silence from a distance. He caused us trouble, even after we imposed the memory block. I had to take a more drastic step."

"Gillings! Yes, I remember now. You are the one who appeared just when we were making progress with Gillings and struck him down. I saw you only for a moment, but I doubt if I'll ever forget how you looked at that moment— poor Gillings..."

"No, you are mistaken. You do me an injustice. Gillings will recover...completely. It was a necessary act. We had to do it to protect ourselves. He saw too much in the vicinity of the ship that night. We had to complete our new fuel research as quickly as possible, without interference from Washington. It is done now...it is all in the past. We have harmed no one seriously."

"I have only your word for that. Is taking a man out into space against his will your way of *not* harming him seriously? If it is, I don't think too highly of it. And your research with the new fuel. You had an accident and some energy seeped out. You might have even been forced to destroy the Earth. That's what we thought in Washington, anyway. Is it true? Was there *that* much danger?"

The Scorpion hesitated a moment, then said with complete candor, "Possibly, but it was a risk we had to take."

For the first time then Lawrence saw the Scorpion in depth, as a strong-willed individual in his own right, distinct from the chill gray anonymity of his race. He stood out clearly, wearing his native costume as gracefully—but not more gracefully—than he had worn the clothing of Earth. But there was a resplendence in his attire now that had been lacking before.

His jacket-like upper garment was silken-textured and midnight blue in color, but when the light struck it, it glimmered with an almost iridescent sheen. From his waist to his sandaled feet the cloth of his trousers seemed molded to his limbs, surpassing in their skin-tight flexibility the tights which athletes wore.

The trousers, too, were of a deep, midnight blue, and were set off by a red-gold sash not unlike a cummerbund. Such a costume might have evoked insulting innuendoes on Earth, but the dignity and assurance with which it was worn dispelled in advance any doubt as to the Scorpion's masculine pride in the wearing of it.

"My name," the Scorpion said, "is D'Qy—Duke. It is always a mistake to dwell with anger or resentment upon the past. What is done is done. We all make mistakes—and the past is a vast graveyard of blunders that can never be repaired. It is a shining storehouse, too, pointing the way to a future that can be changed. Nothing in the universe is so unalterable as the past or so plastic and bright with promise as the future."

"I can believe that," Jim Lawrence said, with sudden, rising bitterness. "The future can be very bright if you are in the saddle. Right at the moment, I don't happen to be."

"You must not think of yourself as a victim, or even as a prisoner," Duke said. There was a grave, pleading urgency in his voice which gave Lawrence pause, making him wonder if he had not perhaps jumped to a premature conclusion concerning the Scorpion's character and intentions.

"I shall try to be brief," Duke went on, his expression so earnest it seemed almost guileless, childlike, in its probing intensity. "We have taken you out into space without securing your consent in advance, and that is certainly an encroachment on your integrity as an individual. I shall be quite frank. It is, in one sense, an act of tyranny.

"But even an act of tyranny can be redeemed by forgiveness freely asked and freely given. I come to you now as a petitioner. I ask forbearance, understanding. We need your help, desperately. My race is facing almost certain destruction—unless you will consent to help us. For many weeks now we have been observing you, studying you. We know you to be a man of exceptional imagination and intelligence."

Lawrence was moved despite himself—not so much by the Scorpion's actual words as by the humility in his voice, his apparent absolute sincerity.

"Let me put it this way. Our race is facing a spiritual crisis. A third of my people have lost—all desire to go on living. And the disease—for it *is* a disease, a malady of the mind and spirit—is spreading. It is spreading so rapidly that in three or four years those of us who find life glorious and rewarding will be in the minority. We will be wanderers and outcasts, hated and feared by everyone, our joy a mockery and a reproach. The living dead will turn on us in fury.

"They will use our joy as a scourge to destroy us—if we do not ourselves succumb to the ghastly malady. Eventually all of us will succumb, unless a cure is found in time."

"But what causes this—this affliction?" Lawrence asked. "You called it a disease. Have you any reason to believe that it is germ carried?"

Duke shook his head, his lips tightening. "No. We are quite sure that it is not caused by any living organism. The victims are disturbed mentally, tormented, in a way that seems to me incomprehensible. To me—because I am not yet one of the afflicted. To them it seems perfectly natural to hate the joy that has made us great as a people. They cover their faces and refuse to speak to us—often even to eat.

"It is, in a sense, a turning away from all human fulfillment. Toward darkness, despair, life-hatred and life-rejection. And that is why we think the affliction is some way profoundly spiritual. It strikes at the very core of being."

"A psycho-analyst might disagree with you," Lawrence said.

"What you call psycho-analysis is to us a science in its infancy," Duke said. "We have explored all of its insights and extended them. We look further—toward eternal laws, universal verities. To us joy is such a verity. It is a biological constant throughout the universe of stars. To experience it in all its richness and fullness is to become almost godlike, and almost one with the eternal. We each carry within ourselves an image that is godlike, and to shatter that image, that vision of joy is to do violence to the laws of our being."

"Why do you need *my* help?" Lawrence asked. "I am not a religious man. I do not even believe—"

"Wait, hear me out. There are many religions on Earth, all different, and I have often thought that each must contain within itself at least a tiny grain of truth, or they would give you no joy at all. Perhaps in one of those beliefs—alien to us—we will find the cure we seek. Perhaps in all of them combined. Or perhaps in what you call metaphysics. Perhaps that tiny grain—no, call it a spark—can be fanned to a healing flame.

"In some ways you are very similar to us. You are a scientific skeptic, and nature to you is a never-ceasing source of joy, the cells of life a mystery that fills you with a contemplative rapture that is not in any way basically different from joy. Intellectual curiosity is the greatest of spiritual gifts, for it mirrors the eternal image I spoke of as clearly as it mirrors that image's counterpart on every planet of every sun.

"That is why we have chosen you. We have chosen five others—from all over Earth. One is an Englishman, a minister of a non-dogmatic, traditionally respected church, another a girl from Washington the third—but you will meet them presently. I have only one thing more to say to you. Try to trust us, to believe in our good faith. Believe that we want only to—to study you, to observe your behavior closely as we seek from you more than we can ever hope to give in return. Be charitable, accept this unfair bargain, and we will withdraw all of our ships from Earth and never cease to be grateful to you."

"But why...why do you wish to study us?"

"Because we all have a reverence for life in our different ways. And the cure, if we find it, will be spiritual in nature. It will have to be. There are two sides to every coin. But our coin has developed a flaw. Part of one face is missing. Your response to our way of life may supply a clue. In your behavior under stress we may see reflected back the part that is missing, the image that must be restored."

Duke laid a firm, reassuring hand on Jim Lawrence's arm. "To you the long journey across space to our home planet will seem like no journey at all. For the light you saw when you approached the ship will gently envelop you again. As I've said, it is an anaesthetic technique, completely harmless, one of our more simple techniques for easing the strain of a journey across thousands of light years.

"You will simply fall asleep and wake up on our home planet. You will be in the midst of a world that will amaze you—a world of Scorpion activity wholly dedicated to joy, to life constantly and creatively renewed, lived to the full, made resplendent by joy.

"You will wake up in a Scorpion city. You will wake up as our guest. The ordeals that you will undergo will be willingly accepted by you...of that I am convinced. We will exert no compulsion. You will see..."

Duke's hand tightened on Lawrence's arm. "Come with me. It is time that you met the others. There is another American...a young lady I met in Washington. She, too, has agreed to help us. Come..."

CHAPTER ELEVEN

LAWRENCE OPENED his eyes on a brightness that half-blinded him, a glimmer so immense that it seemed to fill all space around him. For a moment it remained diffuse, flickering like a gargantuan candle flame, soaring to the perimeter of his vision with darting tongues of blue fire.

Then colors coalesced out of the glare, blues and yellows and purples, melting, running together to form a gigantic semi-circle of wildly shouting men and women—Scorpion men and Scorpion women. Tiers upon tiers of them, extending vertically above him for three hundred feet and then falling away in a sweeping downward curve.

He was in the midst of three hundred thousand spectators, with a frightened Ruth Fraser at his side. She was clutching his arm and staring and he could feel her shivering against him as the shouts rose to a deafening crescendo.

"It isn't a bullfight," she gasped. "It's a slaughter. Each of those Scorpions is walking to their death. They're doing it deliberately. They're hoping to be gored."

"No!" Lawrence scarcely recognized his own voice, so taut was it with emotion and shock. "They can't be that insane."

"But they are. They are, I tell you. Just look at them."

He stared down into the white, circular arena where eight Scorpion matadors were converging on two enraged bulls. They carried no weapons; their breasts were bared to the charge. The bulls were enormous, twelve feet in height, with curving horns that almost met high above their heads.

No such bulls had ever been sired on Earth, or could have survived in competition with the smaller and more agile beasts of a Spanish bullring. But they were agile enough and what they lacked in ground-covering maneuverability they made up for in ferocity and size.

"We were both unconscious when they brought us here," Ruth Fraser whispered, her voice harsh with desperation. "I came to before you did. I saw it all. At first the matadors were armed. They went at those bulls with swords, singing, shouting with joy. They administered a hundred stab wounds and yet the bulls did not go down.

"Now the bulls are at bay, raging, eager to kill. If they wished to live, those matadors should have approached them armed with swords."

"Lances," Lawrence said.

"What?"

"Lances—not swords. They'll be killed, all right. They're not shouting with joy now. Their faces are harsh, fanatical. The life hatred must have come upon them."

Lawrence swayed, running the back of his hand across his forehead, wondering just how much more of this he could stand. The games had been bad enough—the wrestlers, the pole-vaulters, the disc-throwers, the runners, the rapier-parrying youths bent on inflicting a crippling wound.

The spectator sports and the spectator dances. All in the open, under the blazing sunlight—hour after hour, with no rest, no letup. A week of it, under Duke's tutelage. The whirling dances and the community dances, youths and maidens in a frenzy, pirouetting wildly and ever more wildly.

The strain on the spectators was as bad—perhaps worse—than the strain on the contestants themselves. But the Scorpions never seemed to tire of it. They shouted—screamed with joy. With joy, *joy*— How often he had heard that word; what an intolerable mockery it had become.

Was there any joy in watching men die, as the matadors far below were about to die, and even as some of the joyful ones had died, dropping in their tracks from sheer exhaustion and never waking up again.

Was there any joy in surrendering to joy until it killed you?

Someone far below shouted, "The bulls are pain-maddened!"

But Jim Lawrence scarcely heard. He was still in a trance, thinking back, remembering—the lovers. Yes, he had observed them too. All five of the weary, stunned men and women from Earth had been forced to watch the lovers. He had seen the lovers strolling together over garden terraces until they must have grown to hate one another and yet dared not show it, dared not cry out in protest when love had passed its zenith.

He was with Duke again, reliving it all, the days and nights of furious activity. The spectacles, the sports—and the over-crowded living conditions of millions of Scorpions. He could still see their hut-like dwellings in his mind's eye, tucked away in mountain crevices where they could creep out at dawn and welcome the returning sun with shouts of joy, could dance and weave about in circles, arm and arm, until their limbs grew weary and they sank down with the flame of joy extinguished.

"They are merely resting," Duke had assured him. "They will be summoned at noon to the arena or at night to the dances to engage in a further display of joy."

The spectator sports were exhausting, but the participation sports and games were worse. The ten-day bicycle races—and what did it matter if the vehicles were gyroscopic and quite unlike bicycles on Earth—and the wrestling matches that went on for hours and the wild animal baitings, too cruel to have been tolerated on Earth, even if the animals were anaesthetized in the end.

"You will find the hunt exhilarating," Duke had assured him.

The chase, the hunt. There was joy in that, too, beating through jungle brush in pursuit of sabre-toothed cats, with dun-colored flanks and huge, bushy manes. Day after day, night after night, a month of hunting, while the participants sat around campfires singing joyful songs until their voices gave out.

"I did not enjoy it," he had told Duke. "I am glad that it's over."

In a desperate effort to throw off the coiled-spring feeling that was growing, expanding inside his head, pressing outward against his temples, Lawrence forced himself to remember less immediate aspects of the Scorpion civilization—the museums of science and art that he had seen, the schools, hospitals and playgrounds, the bridges and roads, the spaceports, and the vast industrial construction plants.

He recalled the sympathetic eyes of a dark-haired Scorpion woman who had smiled and said, "I doubt if you will ever truly understand us."

But the coiled-spring feeling remained. Everywhere there was a too great brightness, a too complete surrender to joy. Even the sick in the hospitals seemed like joyful children about to be released from school, about to go romping over dandelion-bright meadows the instant the dismissal bell sounded or the teacher turned her back. And the Scorpions in the laboratories and the factories worked without letup, singing, shouting as they labored, giving themselves so exuberantly to their tasks that they wore themselves out.

He could still hear Duke saying, "We do not work to increase wealth. To us work is a creative joy. We would be lost without it."

Everywhere on the planet work had become a creative necessity, work joyfully embraced, but so demanding that it could drive Scorpions—as it certainly would have driven men—to their death. Sports had become a necessity, singing, dancing, the excitements of the chase, taking risks, 'living it up'—and now far below eight Scorpion matadors were walking to their death. The most horrible of deaths—self-impalement, self-immolation—on the horns of enraged and savage beasts.

"The beasts are pain-maddened!" came again from below. "Their charge will be deadly."

From the eight matadors all joy had departed. But for that very reason their self-imposed martyrdom seemed inhuman, unnatural, monstrous and a frightening thing to watch.

Jim Lawrence did not want to watch the matadors die. He covered his face with his hands, and heard only the shouting for a moment, becoming louder and louder. The shouting was no longer joyful. The spectators had become aware of what was taking place and were pleading with the matadors to withdraw before it was too late, to become joyful and exuberantly audacious again.

But even as they shouted they must have known that their pleading would be in vain. There could be no recovery from the blight, the affliction, the life-hatred. When once it took complete possession of a Scorpion there could be no turning back. The arrow of his destiny could point in only one direction—toward a despairing apathy, or self-destruction.

Apathy in some, a more violent urge in others. Not even apathy was completely negative. It could not be sustained without an effort of will—the will to turn one's face resolutely against all joyful effort, all hope, to surrender utterly to despair. Apathy was life-rejection in its simplest form. Self-destruction was its monstrous flowering, the urge full-blown.

"I have been waiting for a moment like this," a calm voice said. "Look down into the area, Jim Lawrence. You are about to witness a tragedy that will seem intolerable to you. But you must look. Unless you do, we will have made no progress. How can I ever hope to understand you as an individual if you are not put, once or twice, to a test such as this? Just how much can you endure? *I must know.*"

Lawrence uncovered his eyes then. But he did not look downward into the arena. He looked instead at the familiar, unbending figure who had materialized out of the shadows at his side.

He said nothing, but his lips tightened and a look of anger—dangerous in its intensity—came into his eyes.

It was Ruth Fraser at his side who spoke. "It is more than I can endure," she said. "Duke...Duke...did you bring me here to make me suffer?"

The Scorpion's hand went out to clasp her arm in a firm, reassuring embrace. At least, it seemed like an embrace, as complete as if he had put his arm around her and drawn her gently to him.

"I would spare you all suffering if I could," he said. "You have suffered too much on Earth. But you two have more inner strength than the others. The five from Earth have collapsed. They have reached the end of their endurance and have turned against me in bitterness.

"They have refused to go on. Each was imaginative and resolute, with great reserves of strength to draw on. But the ordeals they experienced gave them no new spiritual insights, nothing beyond what we already knew. To find a cure we must seek further. We must seek it in you—or in Jim Lawrence."

"Seek it in me, then," Lawrence said. "Let her alone."

The Scorpion's eyes seemed to grow luminous as he returned Lawrence's accusing stare. "She knows that she is free to go," he said. He turned then and spoke directly to Ruth Fraser. "Do you wish to go?"

She shook her head. "No," she said, "I'll stay."

"Watch then. Look down—both of you."

The matadors were within thirty feet of the bulls now, with purple and orange challenge-cloths flung over their arms-colors which, on a planet where bulls grew gigantic in girth, seemed to have a strange power to excite and enrage.

To send a bull charging with a red cloth on Earth was, in itself, no mean feat—for there is nothing in red that excites a bull, if animal psychologists are to be believed. It is the movement, the brightness alone that excites. But here the colors themselves were danger-signals, and when carried by a man or a Scorpion straight toward an already wounded and enraged beast a charge was certain to ensue.

The matadors had spread out a little and were converging in a semi-circle and the foremost was already so near to the most formidable-looking of the two bulls that the animal's wild snortings must have been loud in his ears, the vapor from his breathing a thin spray enveloping him.

Suddenly the bull charged. It pawed the ground once, lowered its head and plunged toward the unarmed, completely defenseless Scorpion, with a bellowing so loud that it could be heard on the highest tier.

The great, almost interlocking horns struck the matador full in the chest. He was lifted up, hurled high into the air and came down with a sickening thud thirty feet from the beast's wheeling bulk.

He lay motionless, his arms outspread, a red stain spreading slowly over the pumice-white arena floor. A shout that was half a groan, full-throated, deafening and incredible in its volume, came from the crowded tiers. It rose and fell in three successive waves, with the almost rhythmic regularity that mass hysteria alone can impart.

And when it dwindled to an agonized murmur the voices of individuals could be heard Scorpion women screaming from tier to tier, Scorpion men shouting to quiet them, or voicing their own horror in stifled moans and barely audible sobs.

"Stop them!" a Scorpion woman screamed. "It isn't too

late! *Kill the bulls!*"

The plea was heeded by someone in authority. A shot rang out, sharp, almost deafening, and one of the bulls toppled to its knees and collapsed forward, its flanks streaked with crimson. But rescue came too late to save all the matadors. Two more were savagely gored and hurled high into the air by the second bull before another bullet could be fired.

The surviving bull's vitality seemed almost beyond belief. Three shots failed to halt it as it charged for a second, and then a third time. It trampled underfoot a matador who had hurled himself toward its lowered horns, ripping the purple-and-orange challenge-cloth to shreds and goring still another Scorpion as it charged straight across the arena toward the spectators in the lowermost tier.

It thudded against the guardrail and recoiled, its horns splintered and dangling, its right leg pawing the ground. It was starting back toward the center of the arena when a barrage of shots brought it down.

Jim Lawrence stirred then for the first time. He had watched the tragedy in complete silence, unable to move or rise, sharing the agony of the matadors, hurt by the cruelty to the bulls and yet realizing that human life came first.

He had watched with a kind of hypnotic detachment, and yet he had felt the terror, the outrage, almost as an affront to himself. His every civilized instinct had been outraged, and he experienced resentment and a desire to forge his indignation and rage into a weapon that he could hurl straight at Duke.

He became aware suddenly that Duke's eyes were upon him, that he was being observed, studied, watched.

"It gave you a great deal of pain, did it not?" Duke asked, in a voice that hardly rose above a whisper. "Pain—and shock. Empathy. You have a great deal of it. You are a man of kindly instincts—you can suffer, feel with and for others. But just knowing that will not help us. There has to be something more."

"Good God!" Lawrence murmured, feeling almost physically ill, his anger ebbing away. "What more do you want? What more could you ask of me?"

"The answer—the cure. I had hoped that in someway you would reveal a *new* emotion…a behavior pattern that only the men and women of Earth would be capable of. There is something we lack and that we hoped you might possess. But I fear our search is to be a hopeless one."

Before Lawrence could reply he became aware that Duke was no longer looking at him, but beyond him. He was staring down at the still form of Ruth Fraser, lying slumped on the cold stone of the tier just beneath the seat that she had occupied with more courage than bodily strength.

"She has fainted," Duke said, bending and gathering her into his arms. "I'm afraid that she, too, is at the end of her endurance. We are alone now, you and I—alone in our search of wisdom, our struggle to solve a dark and almost impenetrable mystery. If we do not solve it the Scorpion image will dim and fade. The mirror of eternity can never grow completely dark, but of the Scorpions…there will be no trace."

CHAPTER TWELVE

THE SCORPION meditation cell was monastic in its simplicity. It contained no furniture and the occupant sat—if he sat at all—upon a stone bench projecting from the wall. He paced—and he usually did pace—across a twelve-foot expanse of weathered stone.

There was one window, very high up in the wall. Beyond it stretched a gray patch of sky. There were no weaving boughs beyond the window, only another gray wall a hundred feet away and splotches of sunlight on that wall.

No snatches of bird-song came from beyond the window, no voices raised in gaiety or made somber by sorrow.

But it was not the silence that made Jim Lawrence bow his head in torment and beat with his fists upon his chest. It was not the silence—but rage.

He had spent less than ten hours in the cell, yet it seemed to him that a lifetime had passed. Not a human lifetime on Earth but the few months that were a lifetime on this planet of no return.

How many questions dared he ask himself, he wondered—how much freedom could he allow himself in his thoughts without running the risk of going stark, raving mad?

Well…he had to make a start. He had to begin somehow, to experiment, to analyze and dissect and define.

Define. Yes, that was a good word, a sound word, a word with a fine, scalpel-like incisiveness to it. Dissect…and define.

Why not start by defining the exact meaning of such semantic imponderables as "civilization"—"progress"—"achievement" and—yes, "endurance."

Start with "endurance"—a word, frequently on Duke's lips. What had enabled him to endure? All of the other words would fall into place, would take on very definite and rewarding meanings if he could answer that one.

What had enabled him to survive, to grip the handrails and hold on? He had watched all of the spectator sports and he'd participated, and the increasing agony of participating, the tension, the whipped-up aliveness, had nearly driven him mad. Yet somehow he'd managed to hang on. How? Why?

Answer that one and you've got the answer to everything, boy.

Think, think hard. Think back to that hunt that was intolerable to you, trailing the beaters, knowing that at any moment a sabre-toothed cat might leap from the underbrush and rend you tooth and claw. The bearers were chanting and singing with joy and you had to pretend to be joyful too. But you were actually as mad as hell.

Why were you mad—so furious? Injustice? Wait now...hold fast to that word. Injustice. The absolute injustice of the hunt in the first place, the unnecessary cruelty of it, its basic absurdity as an outlet for joy.

Defects. There were defects in—hold on now, take a firm grip on that one. There were defects in the whole Scorpion attitude toward joy.

They overplayed it. They forced themselves to be joyful even when they were in danger of losing their lives. They took unnecessary risks to keep that whipped-up emotion always at white heat. The Scorpions had a secret that enabled them to enlarge and enrich human experience beyond anything that had ever been attempted on Earth.

The worship of joy—yes, that was sound, glorious even, as far as joy itself went. But there was another side to the coin. When joy was carried to excess it exhausted itself. There had to be something else—something you could put in its place.

No—that wasn't it, exactly. Not in its place. Something rather that would round it out, supplement it, give it greater scope. Something that would complete the circle, point the way to complete fulfillment. When joy exhausted itself and there seemed to be nothing left—the self-destructive, the life-hating impulses took over.

The Scorpions were an old race. It had taken them perhaps a half million years to exhaust the joy impulse—rather, to carry it to excess and beyond, to complete sterility.

Now the great discovery had lost its savor. It was breaking down everywhere, in the villages, the ten cities, everywhere. All over the planet, life-hatred and apathy and rejection were manifesting themselves.

Duke was, almost certainly, a genius. Was he the guiding intelligence behind the long journey to Earth, in search of an answer—a cure? The missing part of the great, unresolved enigma? It was not too important. Possibly Duke and a dozen other Scorpions. Search the universe. Find a race a little different from ours—a race that may have the answer.

Jim Lawrence imposed a stern discipline on himself, on his thinking. His thoughts were leaping ahead of a most important word, a word that he had gripped firmly for a moment and then released, which was semantically inexcusable.

That word was—*endurance*.

What had enabled him to hang on when the Scorpion worship of joy had seemed to him intolerable? He must think carefully now, analyze his emotions. Wasn't it—anger? Not just ordinary anger, but a burning indignation because the Scorpions seemed to be wearing a blindfold and forcing him along a path that he did not want to take.

Wasn't it because the Scorpions seemed completely unaware of how defective their civilization was in some respects?

All right now. Take a long, steady look at the Scorpion civilization. Its scientific achievements were prodigious, putting to shame the scientific achievements of Earth. In refusing to adopt a routine, utilitarian attitude toward daily living the Scorpions were centuries ahead of Earth. There was no Puritanism in the Scorpion culture, no stiff-necked bowing to taboos.

The Scorpions had the courage to look upon pleasure as a positive good, and love as a positive good—the best things in life. What then was wrong with the Scorpion civilization? In the first place, they did not come to close grips with the more intolerable aspects of community living in a society that was far from completely just.

Why shouldn't the Scorpions be more indignant, angry, disturbed, rebellious? There were intolerable living conditions on the Scorpion planet. The worship of joy, when allowed full scope, resulted in a slave economy. No Scorpion even attempted to be his brother's keeper when all human experience, on an outward plane, at least, seemed dedicated to an almost corybantic abandonment to joy alone.

And there were times when it was necessary for all men—and this applied to Scorpions surely—to be their brother's keeper. Unless they accepted that responsibility all generous emotions, all human compassion, vanished from human life. And the Scorpions were human. Lawrence thought that they were.

And suddenly, in a blinding flash of intuition, he believed he must have the answer. It *was* the answer.

In his wild elation he could scarcely control himself.

Jim Lawrence went to the wall and beat upon it, beat upon the hard stone until his knuckles bled.

"Duke!" he shouted. "Come, let me out. I have the answer, I have the cure!"

CHAPTER THIRTEEN

THE VILLAGE street was completely silent, the small white huts reflecting back the sunlight in thin, wavering shafts that illumined first one despairfully staring Scorpion face and then another. Lawrence and Duke cast long shadows. The instruments they were erecting caused them to intercept the down slanting radiance at a dozen points.

A twenty-foot projection screen had been set up in the middle of the street. Opposite it, on an elevated platform, Lawrence and Duke had erected a complex and elaborate audiovisual instrument, which would throw a series of three-dimensional images on the screen for everyone on the street to see.

The living mummies sat huddled in doorways, not moving at all, their faced blanched, shrunken masks, their eyes glazed and apathetic and not even turned toward the screen.

For fifteen or twenty minutes, while Lawrence and Duke labored to complete their preparations, no one moved or spoke. Then an aged Scorpion—a male—struggled to his feet in one of the doorways and cried out, "Go away. Why did you come here...to torment us? This alien is no friend of ours. Why have you brought him here? For us there is nothing new under the sun...nothing we care about. Go away, depart!"

Duke turned slowly and looked for a moment at the old Scorpion with compassion flaming in his yellow-green eyes. He spoke without raising his voice, and yet his words seemed to carry to the far end of the village street.

"Please be patient," he pleaded. "We have come to help you. We will make no demands upon you. You will see with your own eyes why we have no right to make demands. You will see how blind, self-centered, shortsighted and cruel we have been. Cruel and unjust. What you are about to see is a great evil. We will need your help in correcting that evil. We must all work together to correct it."

He turned back toward Lawrence, who was standing in tightlipped silence by the projection instrument now, his hands busy with the controls.

"All right," Duke said. "We are ready."

Lawrence clicked the instrument on. For a moment there was only a steady, humming sound. Then the great screen became flooded with light and sound and color.

A Scorpion cliff village came into view. For a hundred feet in a vertical direction the sunlight glowed brightly on small, circular huts perched precariously on jagged granite outcroppings that conjured up an image of cruel fingers pointing toward an abyss of emptiness and utter desolation.

A brightness filled the hollows between the dwellings, but beyond there loomed only the gray sky, and a wilderness of rocks and spiny, cactus-like growths that arose starkly from the lengthening shadows.

Then a hut interior came into view. Two young Scorpions lay asleep on a mat of straw, their faces drawn and haggard, their small bodies undernourished. An adult Scorpion came into the hut. He seized the children by the arms and began to shake them. He slapped the face of the male child until his eyes opened in dazed bewilderment.

The two children were taken out of the hut to the edge of the cliff. There they were joined by additional children and other adults. The Scorpions joined hands and began to sing and dance, to weave about in the sunlight.

But there was a weariness on all of the faces, a resentment at being so rudely awakened, and all of the dancers seemed undernourished. The dance became wilder, a torturing nightmare, and suddenly one of the children was screaming.

Jim Lawrence spoke then, for the first time since the

screen had taken on the almost frightening aspect of a reality that seemed somehow even larger and more immediate than life itself, a reality so selective that it resembled more the interpretive vision of an inspired and gifted painter than it did a mere photographic recording in light and sound and color.

"Selectivity is the key," Lawrence whispered to Duke. "A photographic recording can be a work of art, with emotionally shattering overtones. In a moment they should begin to see and to *understand*. Before they merely saw—intolerable living conditions, deprivations, a harshness and an injustice that no one should be called upon to endure.

"The injustice was subconsciously denied or ignored. It was obscured and made to seem sporadic, and almost accidental by the greatness of Scorpion civilization on the positive side—its scientific achievements, its attitude toward daily living."

"Yes..." Duke said. "Yes, I know. And it is a society I still believe in because I know all life is imperfect and that the greatest of wrongs can be set right."

"They can be," Lawrence said, "if emotional shock, the emotional awakening, can be made profound enough. That's my sole purpose now and why we've worked so hard these past few days together. I hope this presentation awakens your people. I must rip away the blindfolds they have drawn over their eyes. It's only human not to want to understand anything that seems too frightening. We all seek to hide truths which will shatter the belief in social justice instilled in us in our infancy...our faith in the complete goodness, the complete rightness, of our own way of life.

"They've never before had the darker side of Scorpion society presented to them in quite this way, as a dramatic human tragedy unfolding directly before their eyes, stripped of all non-essentials, made compelling and selective by deliberate design. Earth's greatest playwrights—Sophocles,

Shakespeare—had the genius always to create such an illusion. They knew how overpowering a performance on a lighted stage could be...how in the theatre each actor becomes an eloquent and moving figure, enlarged by spectator identification far beyond the dimensions of ordinary life.

"Have patience now, wait. These recordings should be cumulative in their emotional impact. In a moment they should begin to experience the first stirrings of understanding, of anger. And when they do—"

The cliffside scene had faded from the screen and another was unfolding. A dozen Scorpion adults were laboring over complex-looking tools and instruments in an industrial assembling plant. They were singing as they worked, but they did not appear to be singing inwardly. Their faces were as drawn and haggard as the faces of the sleeping children had been.

Suddenly one of the Scorpion workers bent and set in motion an odd-looking instrument with a projecting metal hood that gleamed dully in the overhead light. Beneath the hood there was a bright and continuous flashing. The Scorpion adjusted the instrument carefully while he continued to sing, regulating its power-flow, slowing it down and speeding it up. Then something distracted his attention for a moment. He looked up quickly, and as he did so his hand moved dangerously close to the flashing.

He leapt back with an agonized scream and then stood utterly motionless, staring down in horror at the gleaming red stump where his hand should have been. The instrument slowed and the sharp, scissor-like blades that had taken away his hand ceased to rotate.

Instantly everyone in the plant stopped singing.

The scene vanished and the bullfight that Lawrence had witnessed filled the screen... The deafening shouts, the gored matadors, the enraged and charging beasts—came into the village street, and remained for ten full minutes. It was brighter, more terrifying than the original spectacle had been. After that—silence.

The screen went blank and no one spoke for a moment.

Then the Scorpions who sat huddled in the doorways began to whisper among themselves. It was a low murmur at first, a barely audible undercurrent of sound on cracked and shriveled lips. Then, quite suddenly, a Scorpion woman cried out in torment. She had visualized torment and tragedy. She was feeling resentment, anger—for the first time.

The words were almost a scream, high-pitched, trailing off into unintelligibility. "Don't know how I stood it...don't know...don't know..."

Another woman's voice arose in bitter protest. "Those poor children! Did you see their faces—the wretchedness in their eyes? They were forced to dance and sing when they were weak with hunger. Hunger or neglect—a cruel indifference. They wanted only to sleep. You could see that."

A male voice demanded, "How could we have been so blind? Where were our eyes? We have laws that prohibit children from working in industry. But there is little joy left in any of our children. We force them to be joyful when they wish only to play simple games, wish only to be carefree and well nourished. You cannot force joy upon children. They are naturally joyful, if you are not cruel to them.

"It was *there, all the time* this cruel thing, this injustice. But we did not see it. Why did we not put an end to it? Why did we not walk the roads in protest? We turned our faces from joy because we were weak, and blind and afraid. We gave up the struggle, we buried ourselves alive. We could have protested, but we did nothing."

A young male Scorpion, so gaunt and emaciated that his

body seemed a mere shriveled husk over protruding bones, cried out in bitter self-reproach, "Yes, yes—that is true. We did not want to go on living. But we had no right to make such a decision when there were so many who needed us, so many who lacked even our inner strength...the wretched and the helpless."

A young Scorpion woman whose face, despite its gauntness, still retained a vestige of youthful beauty, rocked slowly back and forth, sobbing, "I could not look at those charging bulls. The cruelty...the brutality was more than I could bear. We are all guilty. We allowed ourselves to become callous, we accepted without question the cruel lies we had been taught to believe. I wanted to tear my garments in shame. I only saw the joy before—now I know it was destruction."

The old Scorpion who had spoken in anger while Duke had been assembling the projection instrument had sat tight-lipped in the doorway of his hut and refused at first even to look at the screen. But during the bullfight scene he *had* looked, and now he arose to speak again.

"We must put an end to the cruelty," he said, with a different kind of anger. "We must work together to build a better world."

Up and down the streets his words were caught up and repeated. From lip to lip the defiant cry passed...from living mummy to living mummy. But they were no longer mummies now. Their lethargy, their life-hatred, was gone.

There was silence again for a moment. Then Duke spoke without raising his voice and yet his words were heard distinctly by everyone.

"Yes...I think we have found the answer we have been seeking. I think we have found the cure. You have something to live for now, something to replace the bleak emptiness and give new meaning, new direction to your lives.

But the struggle will not be easy and it will go on for as long as we exist as a people. We have not yet, despite all of our gains, conquered poverty, disease, human ignorance and stupidity. There will be more schools to build, more research to conduct, more battles to be fought with those who have set their faces resolutely against change.

"We must be fearless in our search and when joy exhausts itself and becomes an intolerable burden we must put it aside, knowing that you do not destroy a shining garment when you take it off and place it, neatly folded, in a chest.

"There is another garment that we must wear at times and rejoice because we are privileged to put it on. It is the garment of social justice and social change, and it must be spread wide enough to cover everyone, to cover all of the growing needs of a growing society until we stand together in complete solidarity under the stars."

He turned to Jim Lawrence then and said, quite simply, "You are a very good diagnostician. But I'm afraid that I cannot repay you as you would repay a wise physician on Earth. When the services rendered are very great, payment becomes impossible." He nodded, standing very still...very straight.

"I don't think your hypothetical physician would mind at all," Lawrence said, warmed by the radiance of Duke's smile. "All I ask is to be taken back to Earth."

Duke said, "Yes, I thought you would make that request. Well...there is one who is staying because she wants to stay. I am hoping that she will never change her mind."

"I don't think she will," Lawrence said.

EPILOGUE

THE SCORPION SHIP passed slowly above the golden dome of the Capitol, encircling the long avenues of cherry trees in bloom and the crowds who had assembled without fear to watch its almost miraculously maneuvered descent.

It came to rest on a level lawn close to the Lincoln Memorial and from the shining central port a Scorpion and a man emerged and stood quietly awaiting the arrival of the delegates from the Great Powers and the small nations.

The long journey through space had not even dulled the glimmer on the smooth, cylindrical hull. And the messages sent ahead during the last stage of the journey seemed to blend with that glow and become a part of it...so that no one doubted the words that had come winging through space a week before the returning ship had been sighted on Mount Palomar.

"We will share with you all of our knowledge...all of our gains. Before we depart your technology will equal ours and there will be a free interchange of ideas between us. All barriers will be dissolved. For as long as you wish we will communicate freely together. Our mission on Earth has been successful and there is no need for us to search further. All of our ships will be withdrawn.

"We will not return unless you request us to do so...as freely invited guests and goodwill ambassadors, as journeymen scientists, as fellow-wayfarers on the long journey...'to follow knowledge like a shining star.' And you will be warmly welcomed, always, when you visit us in return."

On the wide, green lawn, between the stately trees, a strange peace and serenity seemed to filter down with the sunlight, touching each bough in a subtle and gradual way, until all things grew quiet. It was almost as if in some extraordinary manner, the ship itself had become enveloped in a phantom aura of green.

Beneath the central port Duke turned to the man at his side and said: "When I address the United Nations I will feel a little more at ease if you are on the platform beside me, Jim Lawrence. Will you be?"

The quick, reassuring response in the level eyes confronting him left no room for doubt on that score.

THE END